ROBERT LOUIS STEVENSON'S

TREASURE ISLAND

by Robert Louis Stevenson
retold by Wim Coleman and Pat Perrin
illustrated by Greg Rebis

Librarian Reviewer
Allyson A.W. Lyga MS
Library Media/Graphic Novel Consultant
Fulbright Memorial Fund Scholar, author

Reading Consultant
Mark DeYoung
Classroom Teacher, Edina Public Schools, MN
BA in Elementary Education, Central College
MS in Curriculum & Instruction, University of Minnesota

Graphic Revolve is published by Stone Arch Books
151 Good Counsel Drive, P.O. Box 669
Mankato, Minnesota 56002
www.stonearchbooks.com

Library of Congress Cataloging-in-Publication Data
Coleman, Wim.
     Treasure Island / by Robert Louis Stevenson; retold by Wim Coleman and Pat
Perrin; illustrated by Greg Rebis.
     p. cm.—(Graphic Revolve)
     ISBN-13: 978-1-59889-050-1 (library binding)
     ISBN-10: 1-59889-050-6 (library binding)
     ISBN-13: 978-1-59889-222-2 (paperback)
     ISBN-10: 1-59889-222-3 (paperback)
     1. Graphic novels. I. Perrin, Pat. II. Rebis, Greg. III. Stevenson, Robert Louis,
1850–1894. Treasure Island. IV. Title. V. Series.
PN6727.C5725T74 2007
741.5'973—dc22   2006007695

Summary: Young Jim Hawkins discovers an old treasure map and sets out on a
harrowing voyage to a faraway island. The violent sea is just the first of many
obstacles, as Jim soon learns there are dangerous men seeking the same treasure.

Credits
Art Director: Heather Kindseth
Graphic Designers: Heather Kindseth and Kay Fraser
Colorists: Greg Rebis, Dylan Edwards, Tiffany Moore,
Leila Hill, Melissa Armstrong and Katherine Rebis

1 2 3 4 5 6 11 10 09 08 07 06

Printed in China

TABLE OF CONTENTS

INTRODUCING . . .

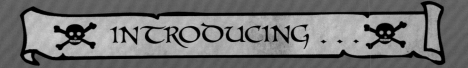

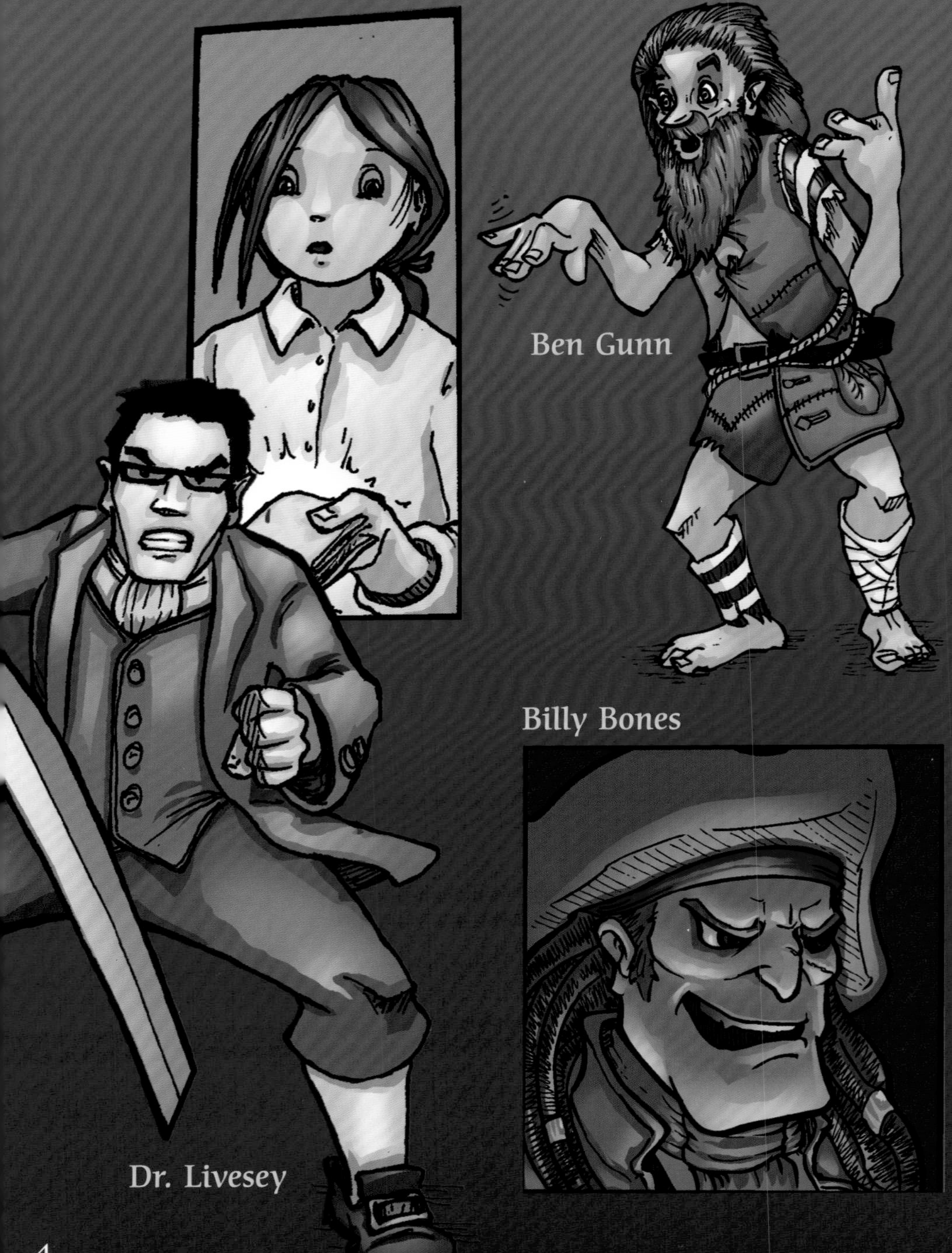
Jim Hawkins
Ben Gunn
Billy Bones
Dr. Livesey

Mr. Trelawney

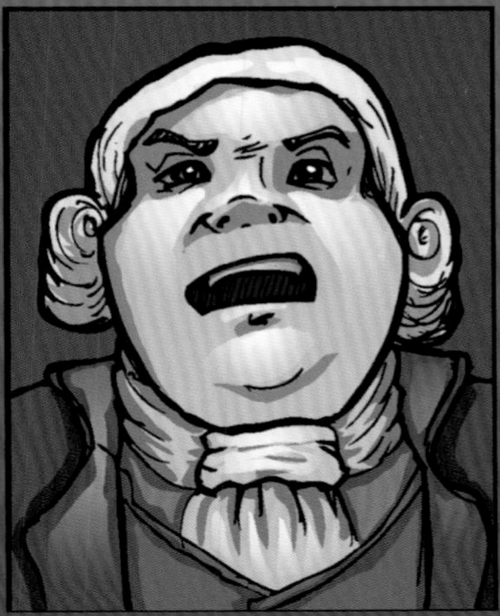

Captain Smollett

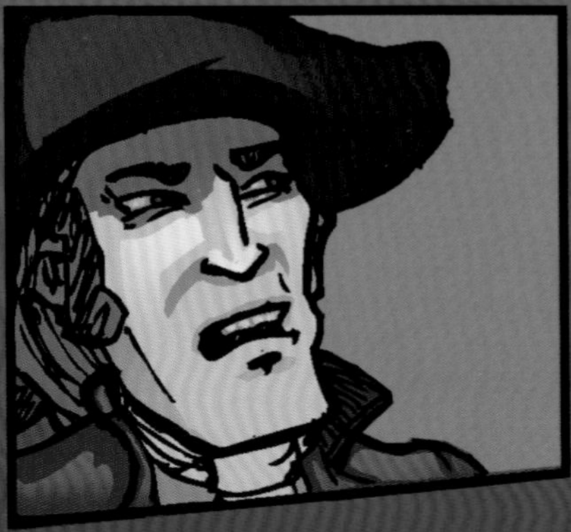

Long John Silver

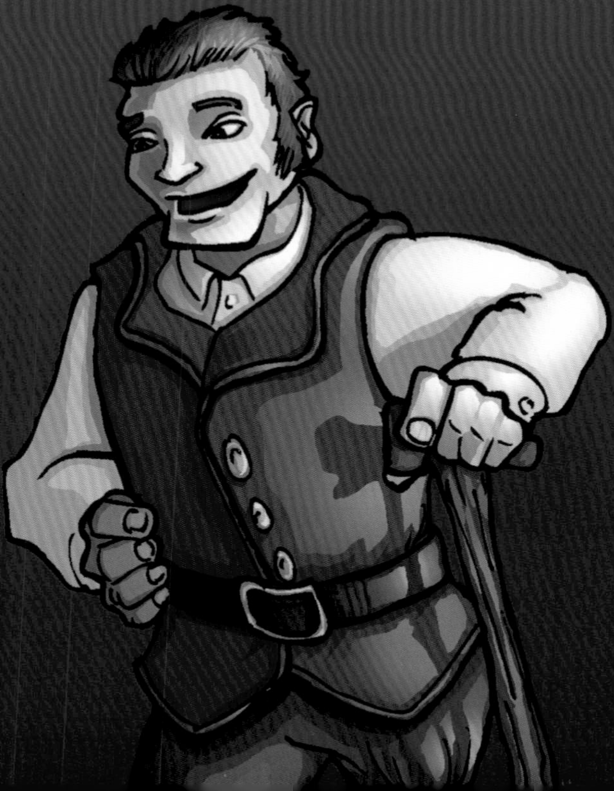

Israel Hands

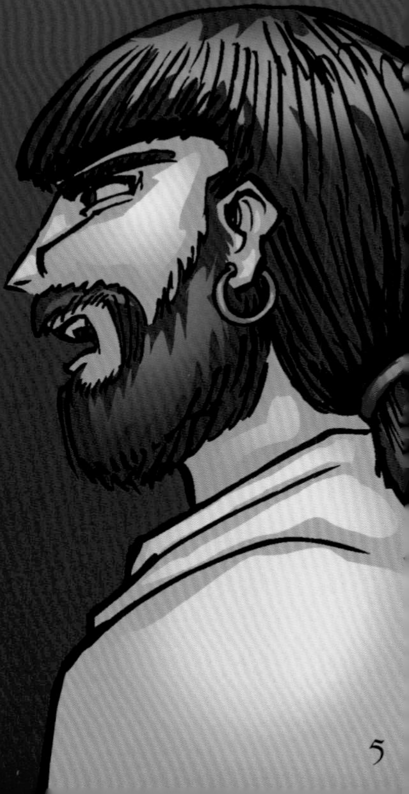

CHAPTER 1 The Old Sea Captain

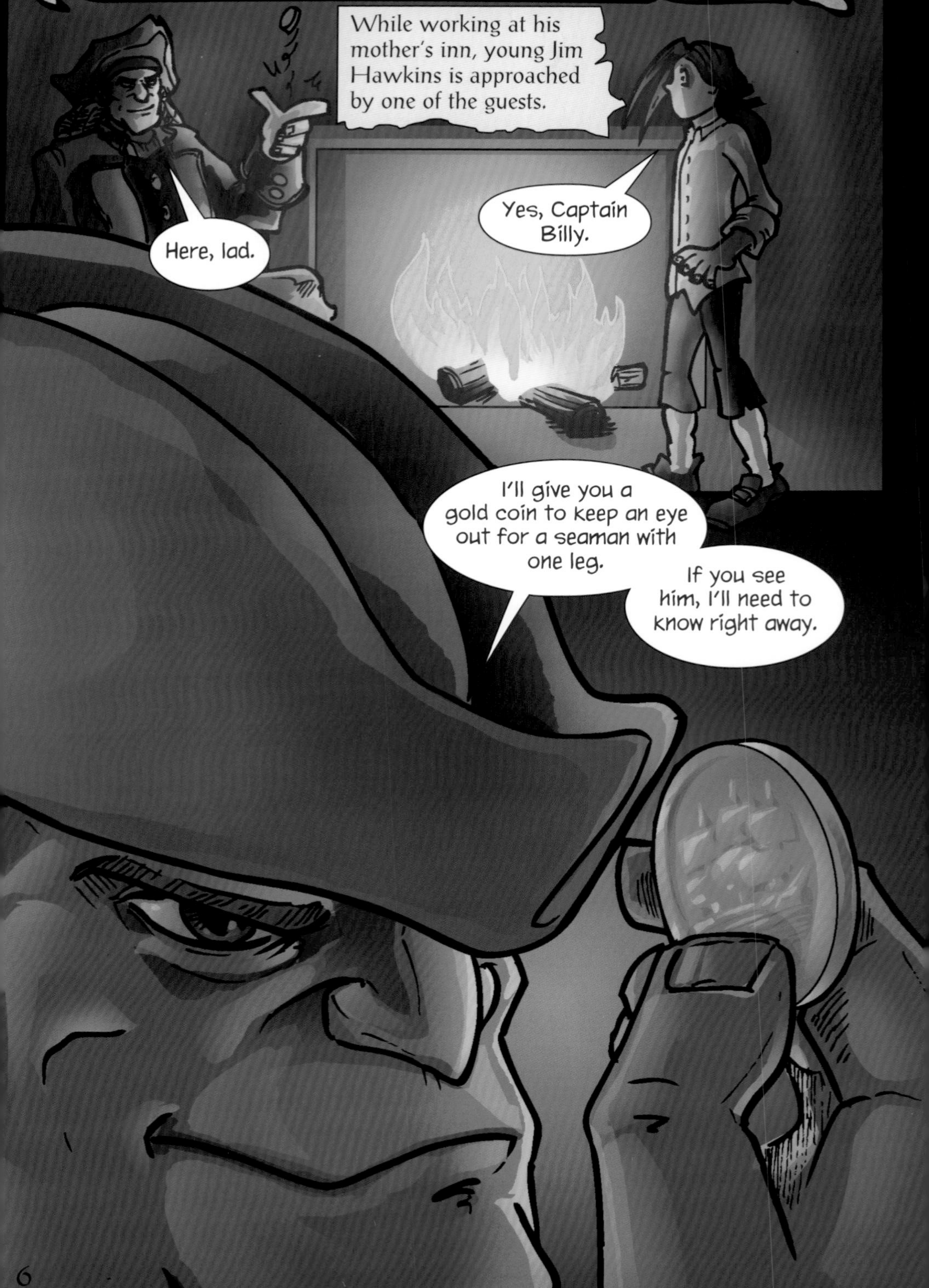
While working at his mother's inn, young Jim Hawkins is approached by one of the guests.
Here, lad.
Yes, Captain Billy.
I'll give you a gold coin to keep an eye out for a seaman with one leg.
If you see him, I'll need to know right away.

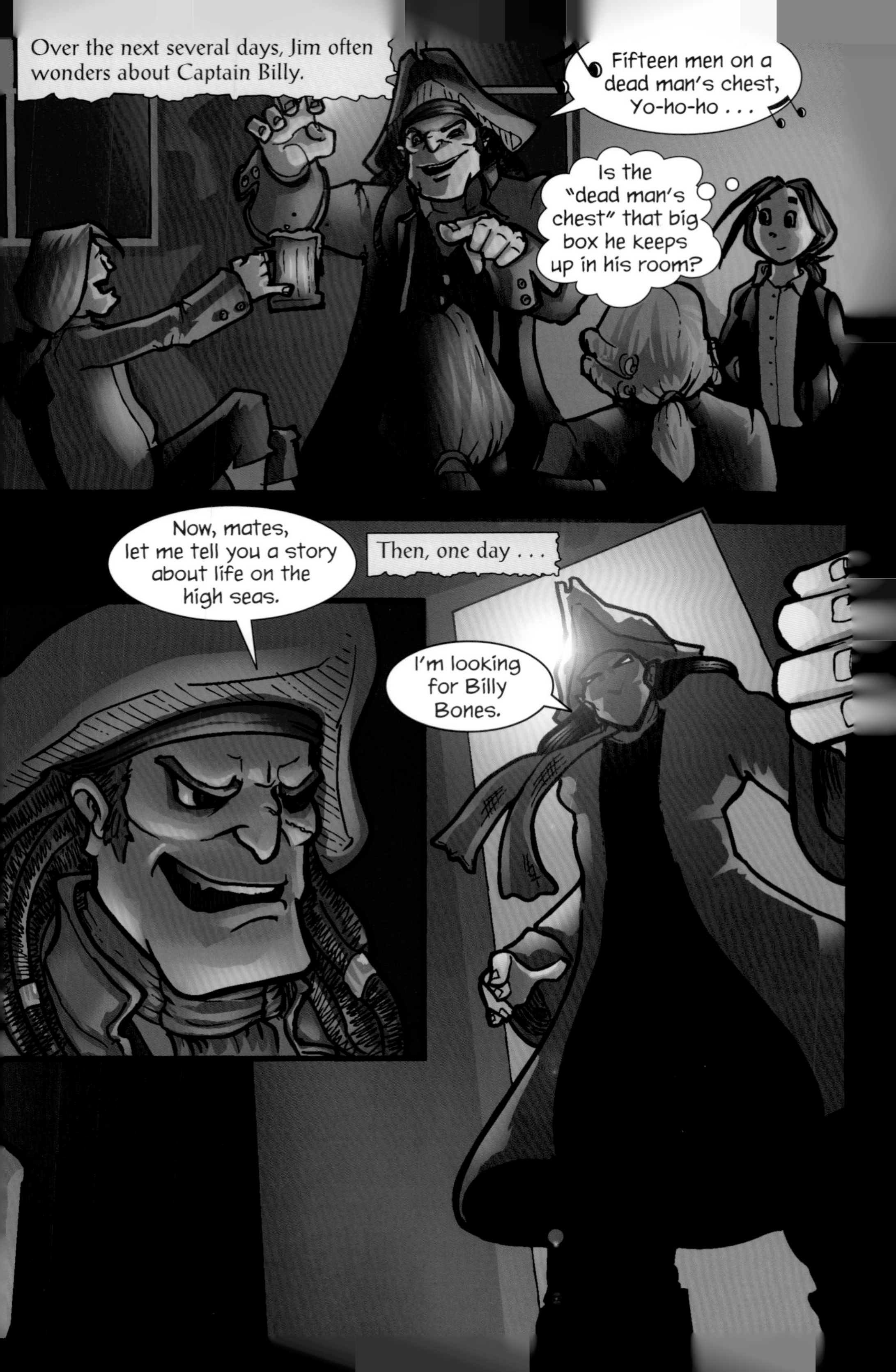
Over the next several days, Jim often wonders about Captain Billy.
Fifteen men on a dead man's chest, Yo-ho-ho . . .
Is the "dead man's chest" that big box he keeps up in his room?
Now, mates, let me tell you a story about life on the high seas.
Then, one day . . .
I'm looking for Billy Bones.

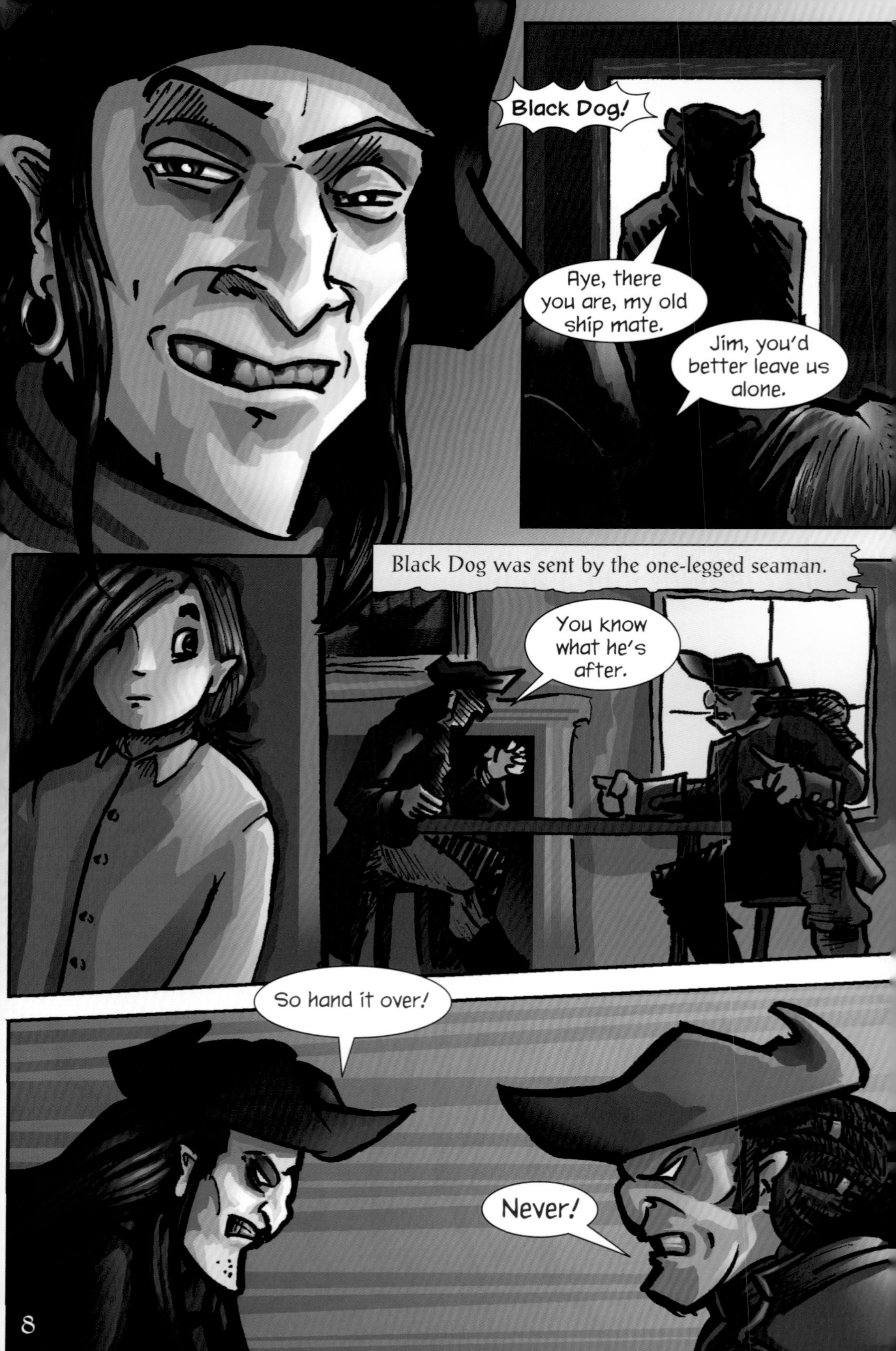
Black Dog!
Aye, there you are, my old ship mate.
Jim, you'd better leave us alone.
Black Dog was sent by the one-legged seaman.
You know what he's after.
So hand it over!
Never!

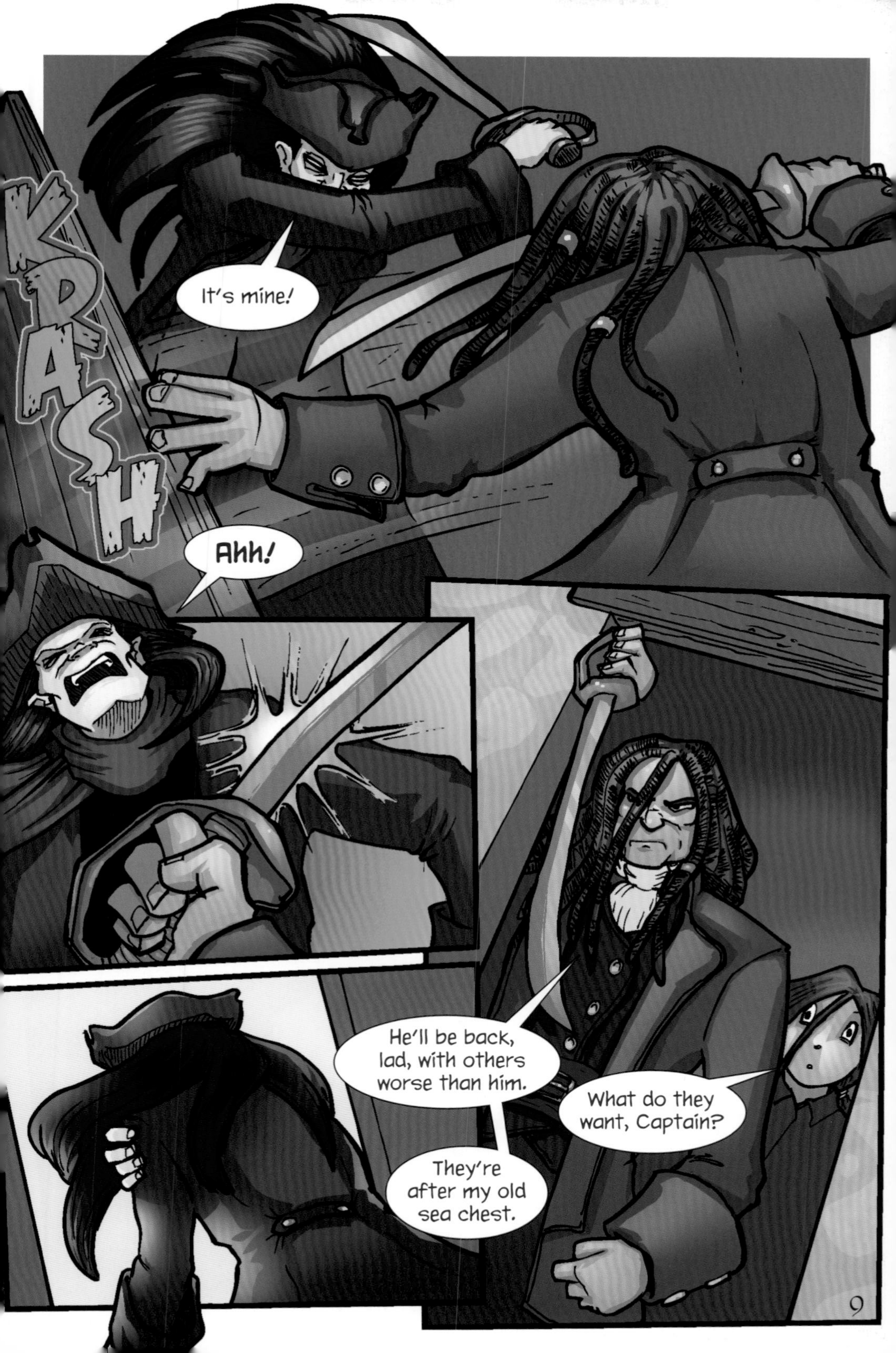

It's mine!
KRASH
Ahh!
He'll be back, lad, with others worse than him.
What do they want, Captain?
They're after my old sea chest.

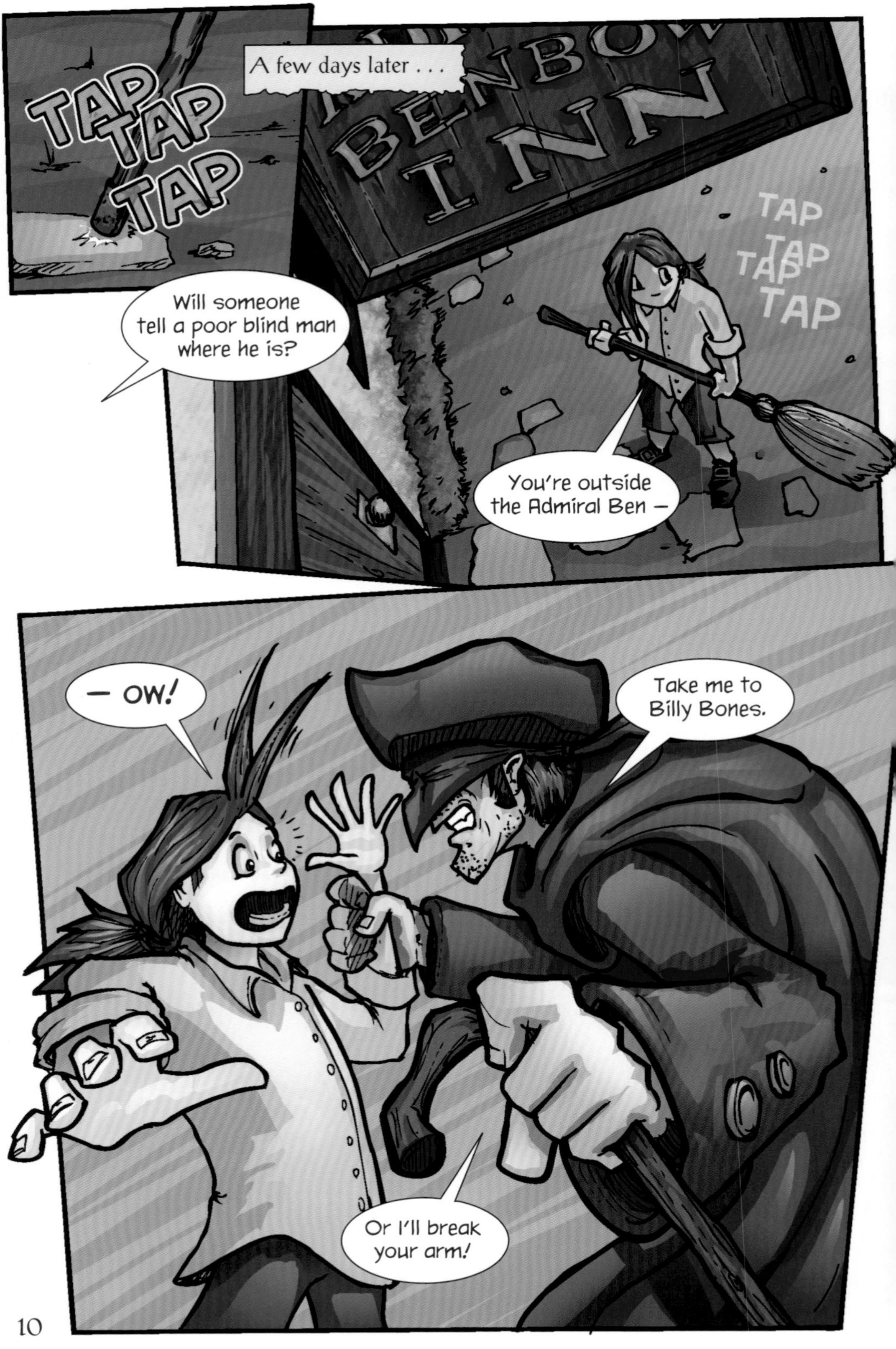
TAP TAP TAP
A few days later . . .
BENBOW INN
Will someone tell a poor blind man where he is?
TAP TAP TAP TAP
You're outside the Admiral Ben –
– OW!
Take me to Billy Bones.
Or I'll break your arm!

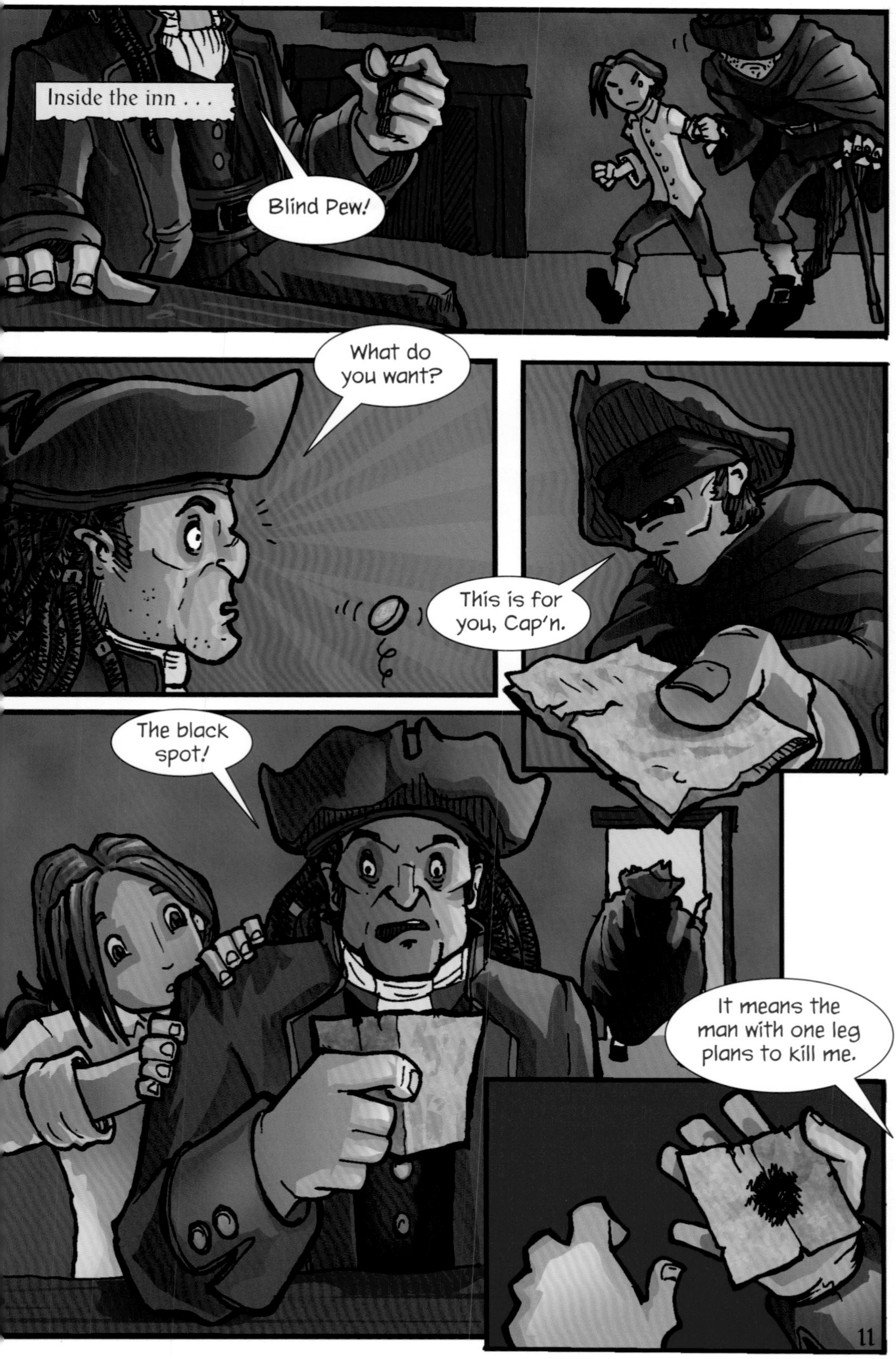

Inside the inn . . .
Blind Pew!
What do you want?
This is for you, Cap'n.
The black spot!
It means the man with one leg plans to kill me.

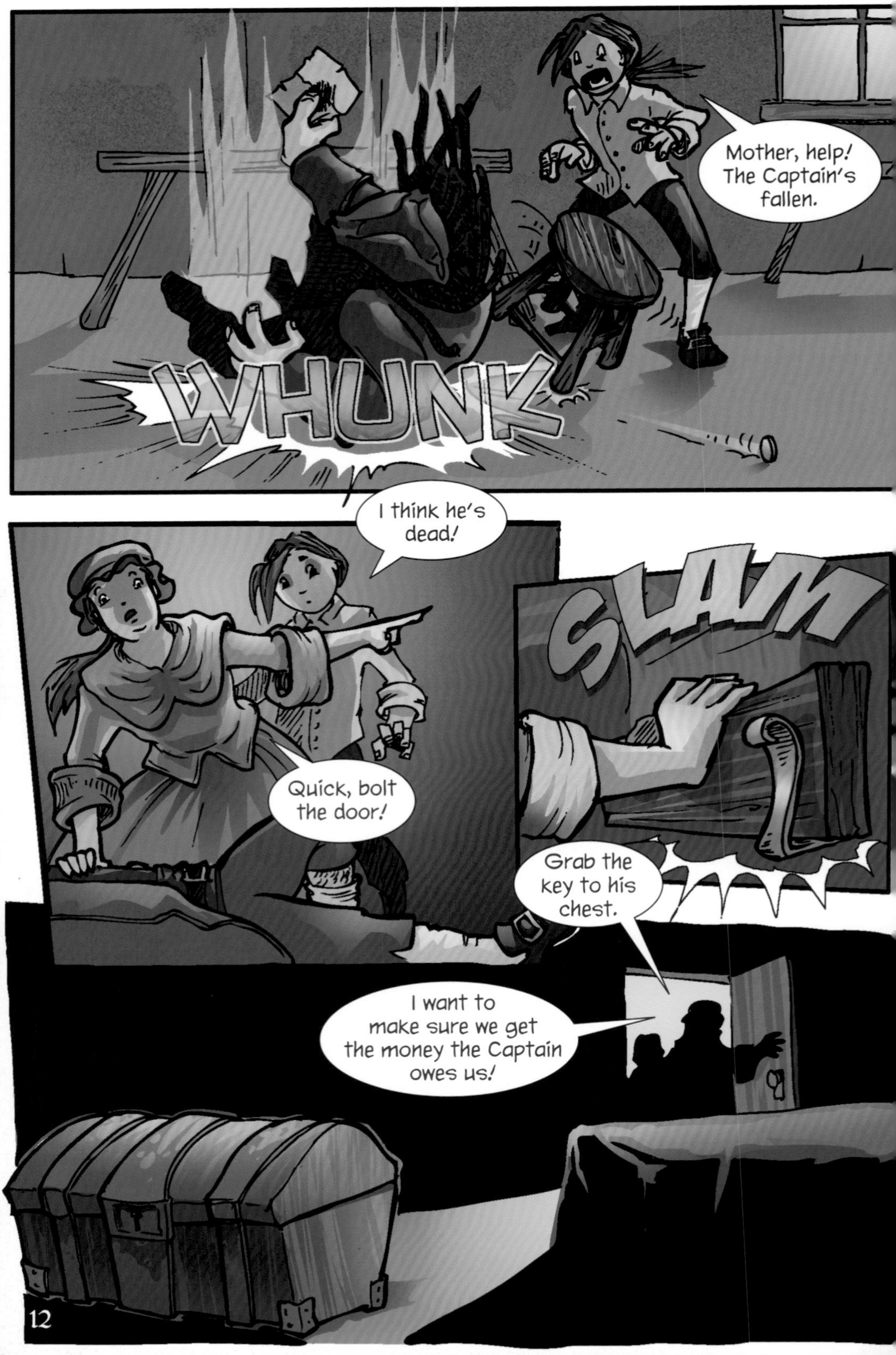
Mother, help! The Captain's fallen.
WHUNK
I think he's dead!
Quick, bolt the door!
SLAM
Grab the key to his chest.
I want to make sure we get the money the Captain owes us!

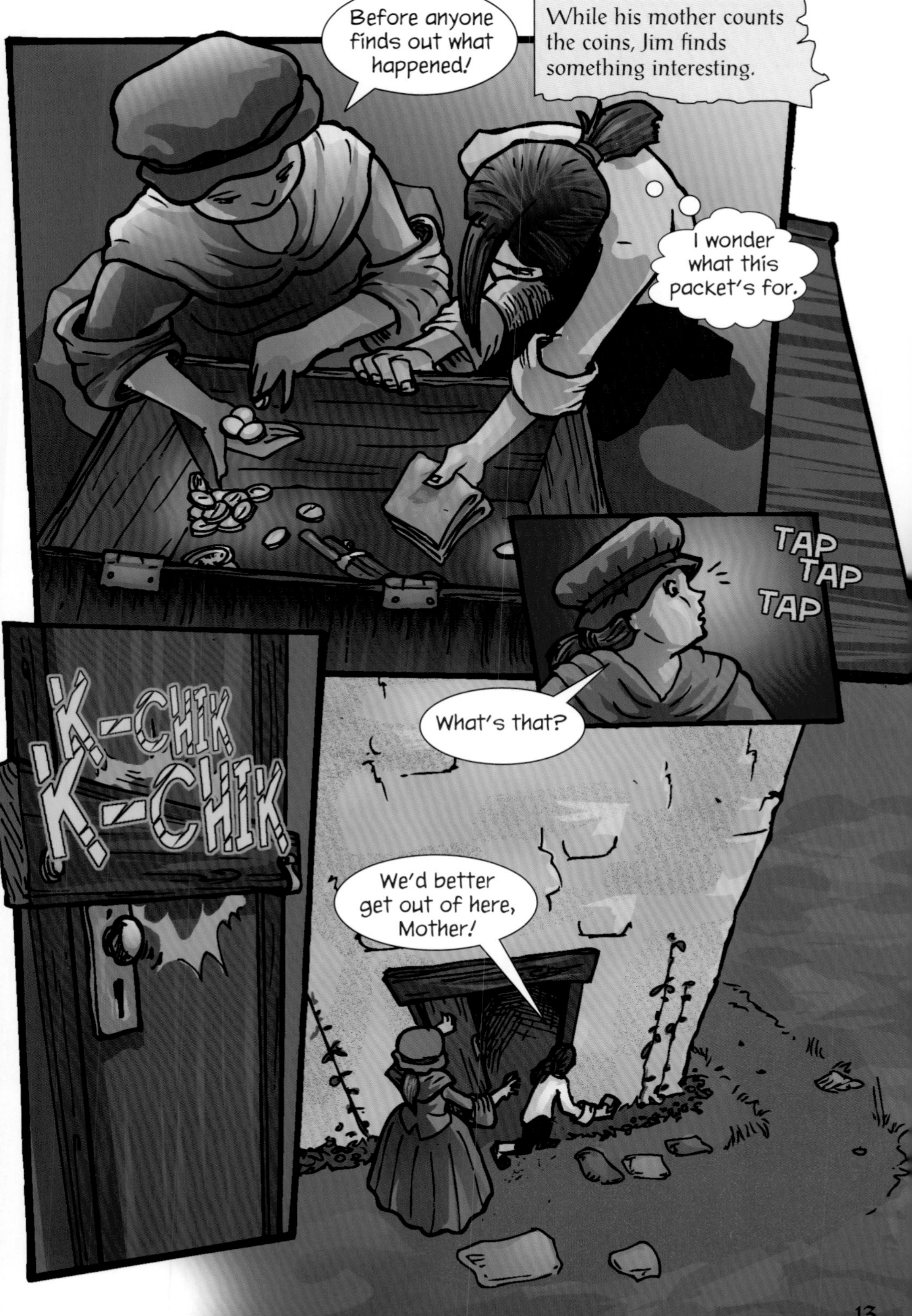

Before anyone finds out what happened!
While his mother counts the coins, Jim finds something interesting.
I wonder what this packet's for.
TAP TAP TAP
What's that?
K-CHIK K-CHIK
We'd better get out of here, Mother!

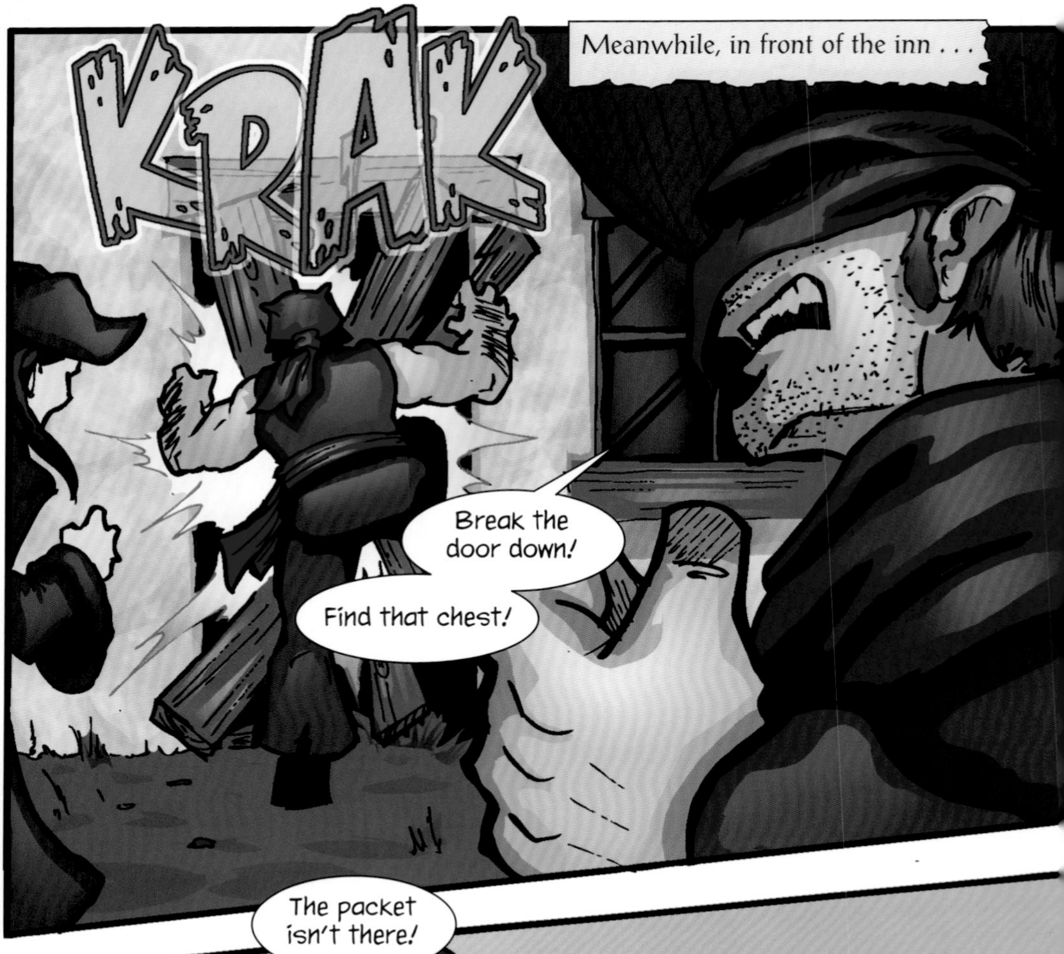
Meanwhile, in front of the inn . . .
KRAK
Break the door down!
Find that chest!

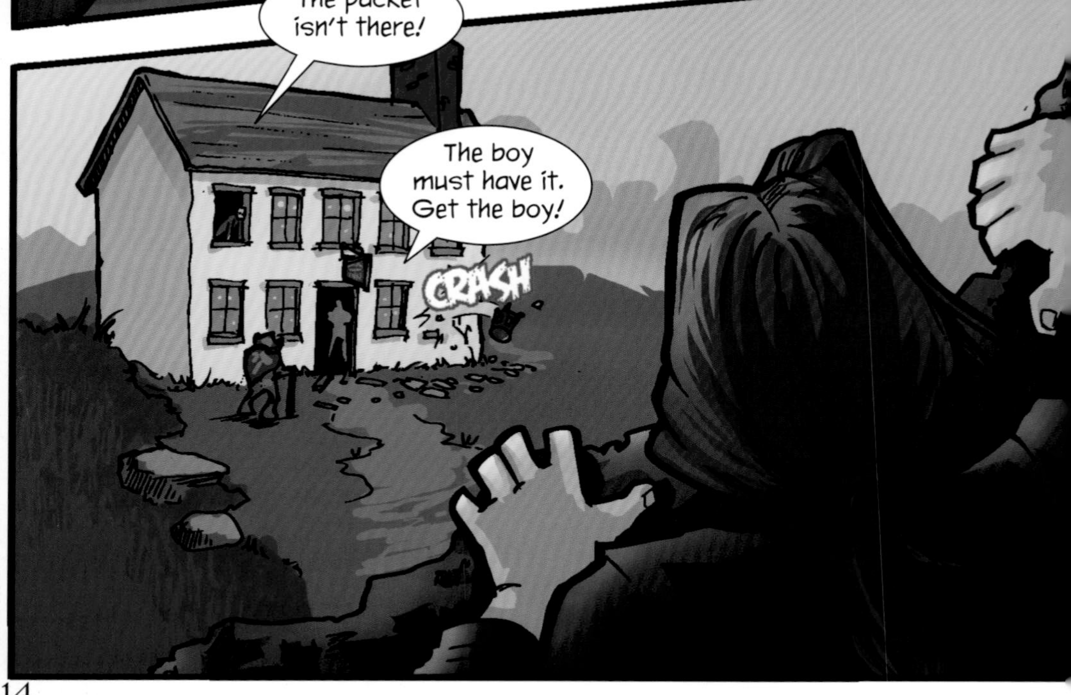
The packet isn't there!
The boy must have it. Get the boy!
CRASH

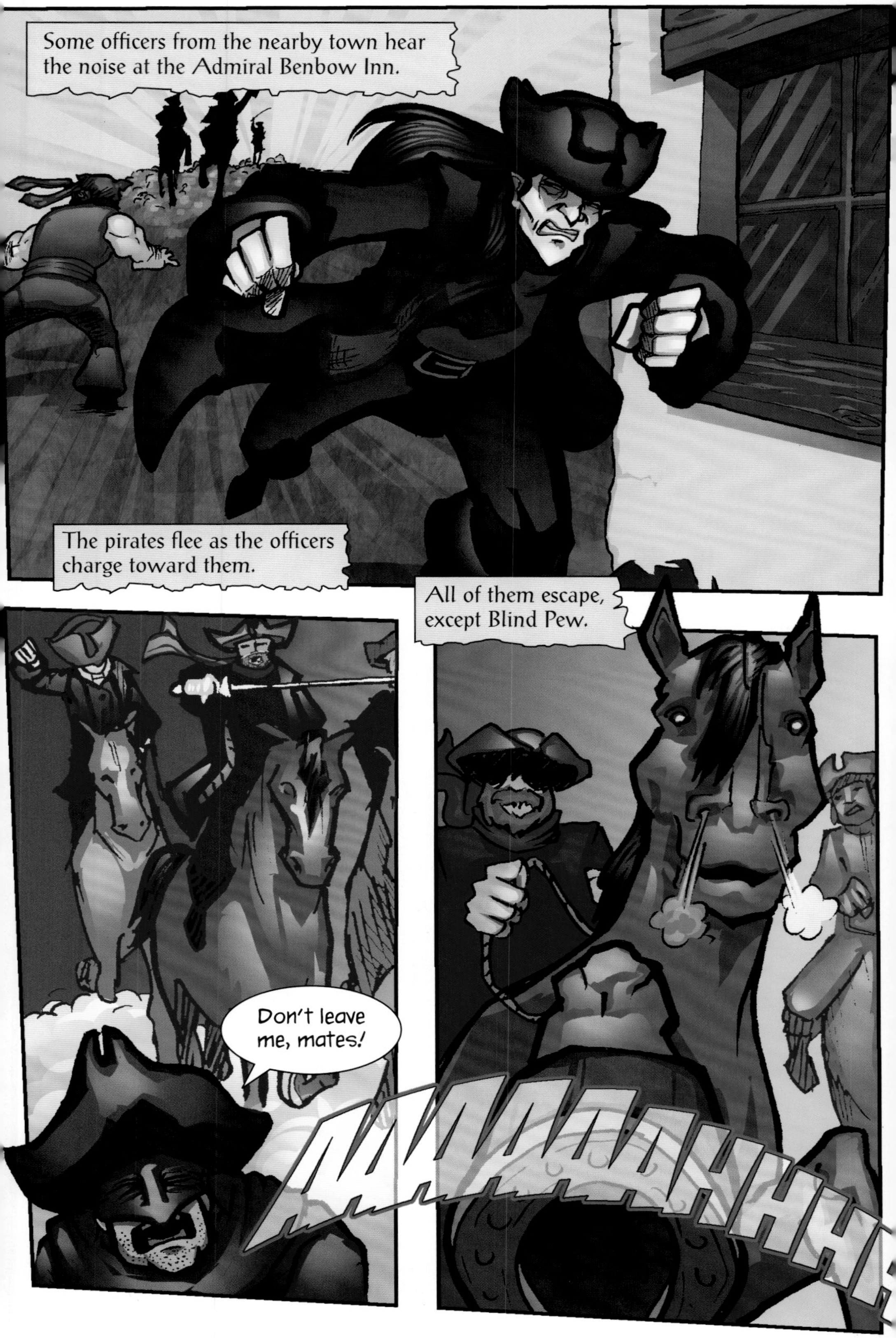
Some officers from the nearby town hear the noise at the Admiral Benbow Inn.
The pirates flee as the officers charge toward them.
All of them escape, except Blind Pew.
Don't leave me, mates!

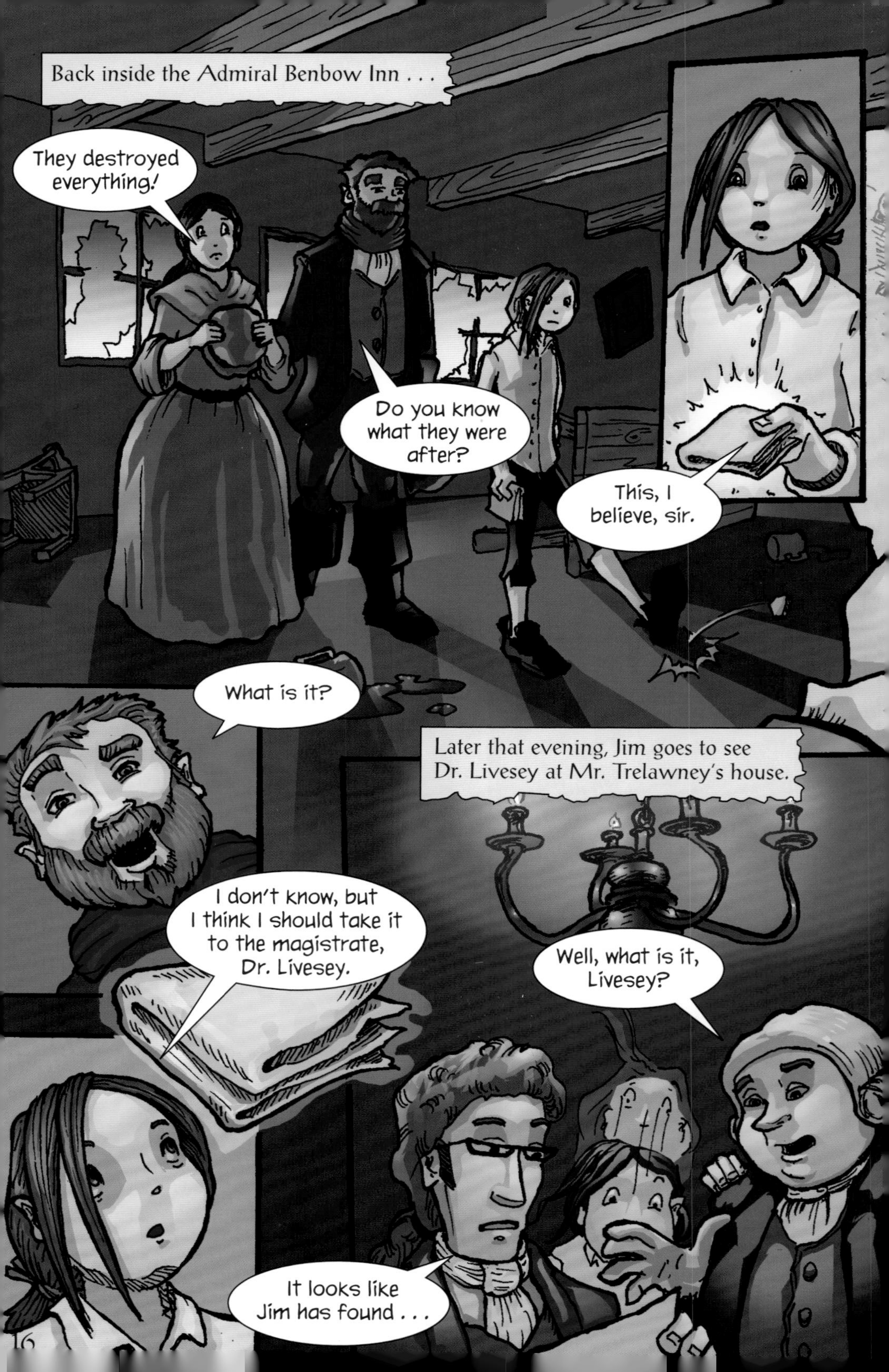

Back inside the Admiral Benbow Inn . . .
They destroyed everything!
Do you know what they were after?
This, I believe, sir.
What is it?
I don't know, but I think I should take it to the magistrate, Dr. Livesey.
Later that evening, Jim goes to see Dr. Livesey at Mr. Trelawney's house.
Well, what is it, Livesey?
It looks like Jim has found . . .

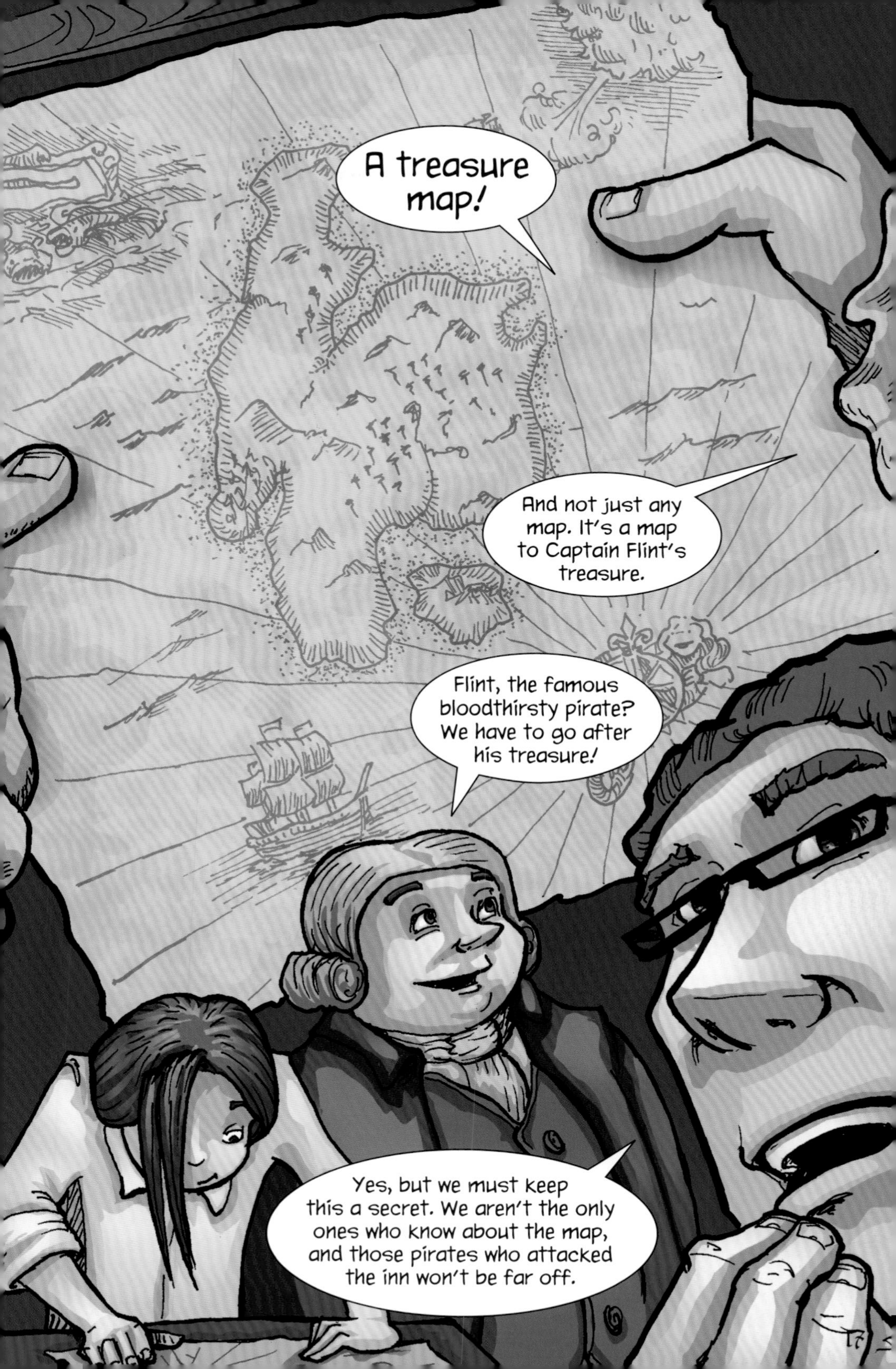
A treasure map!
And not just any map. It's a map to Captain Flint's treasure.
Flint, the famous bloodthirsty pirate? We have to go after his treasure!
Yes, but we must keep this a secret. We aren't the only ones who know about the map, and those pirates who attacked the inn won't be far off.

CHAPTER 2 The Sea Cook

Mr. Trelawney leaves to buy a ship. A couple of weeks later, he sends for Jim to come to Bristol, England.

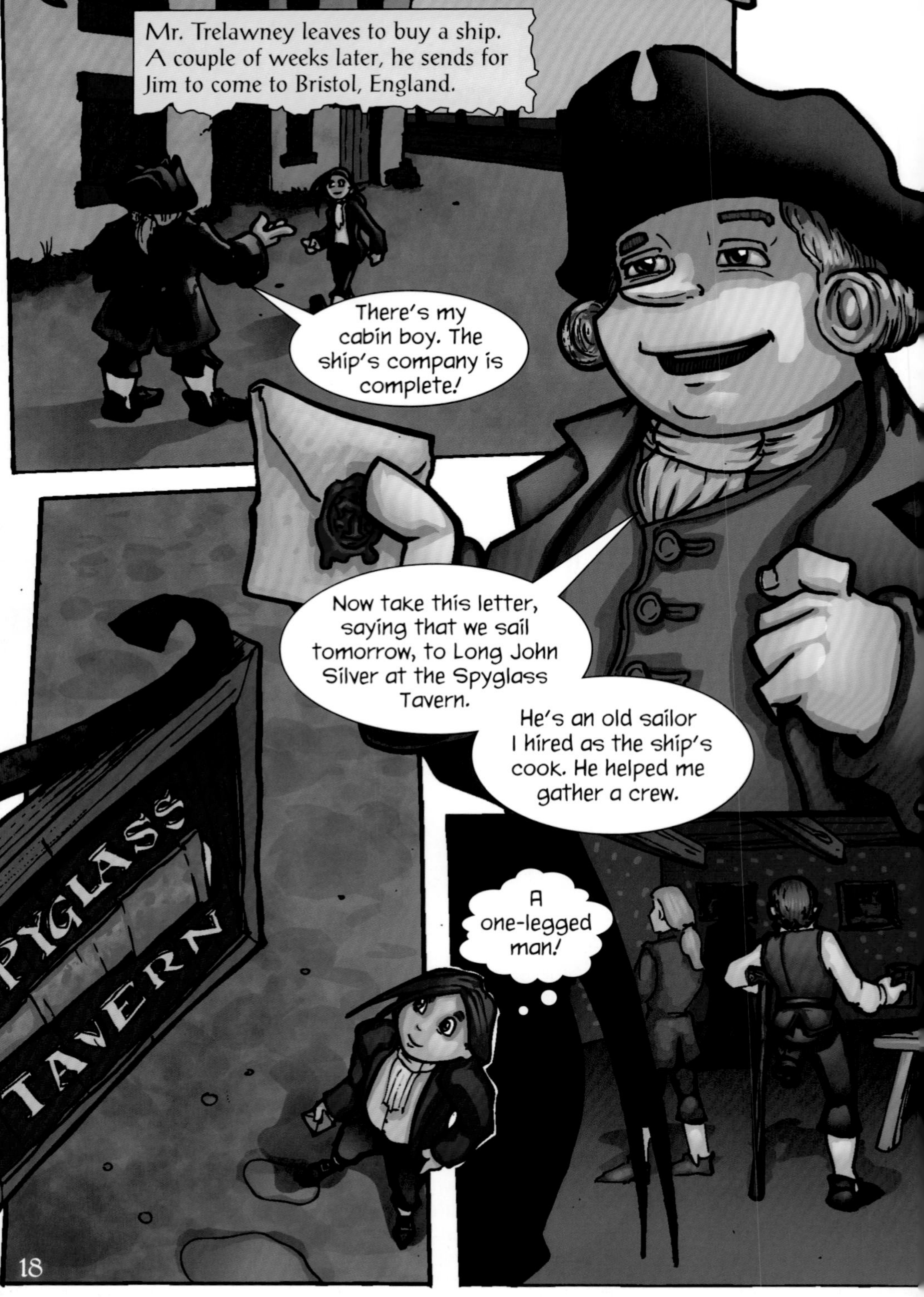

There's my cabin boy. The ship's company is complete!
Now take this letter, saying that we sail tomorrow, to Long John Silver at the Spyglass Tavern.
He's an old sailor I hired as the ship's cook. He helped me gather a crew.
SPYGLASS TAVERN
A one-legged man!

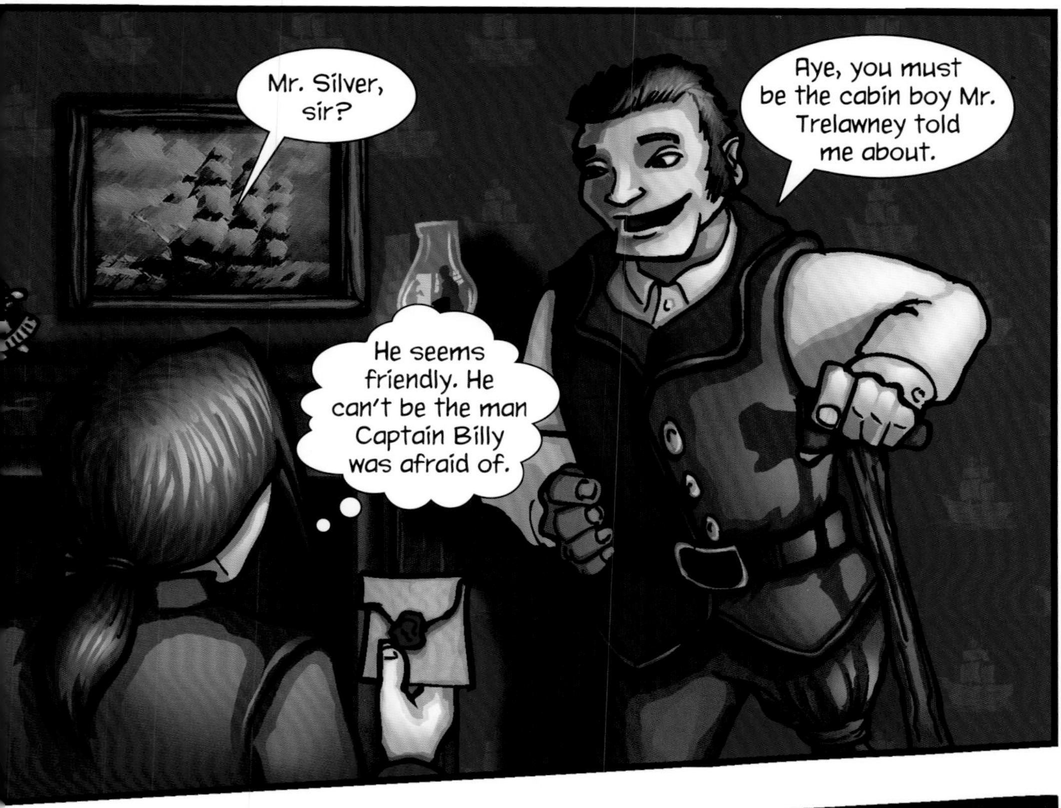
Mr. Silver, sir?
Aye, you must be the cabin boy Mr. Trelawney told me about.
He seems friendly. He can't be the man Captain Billy was afraid of.

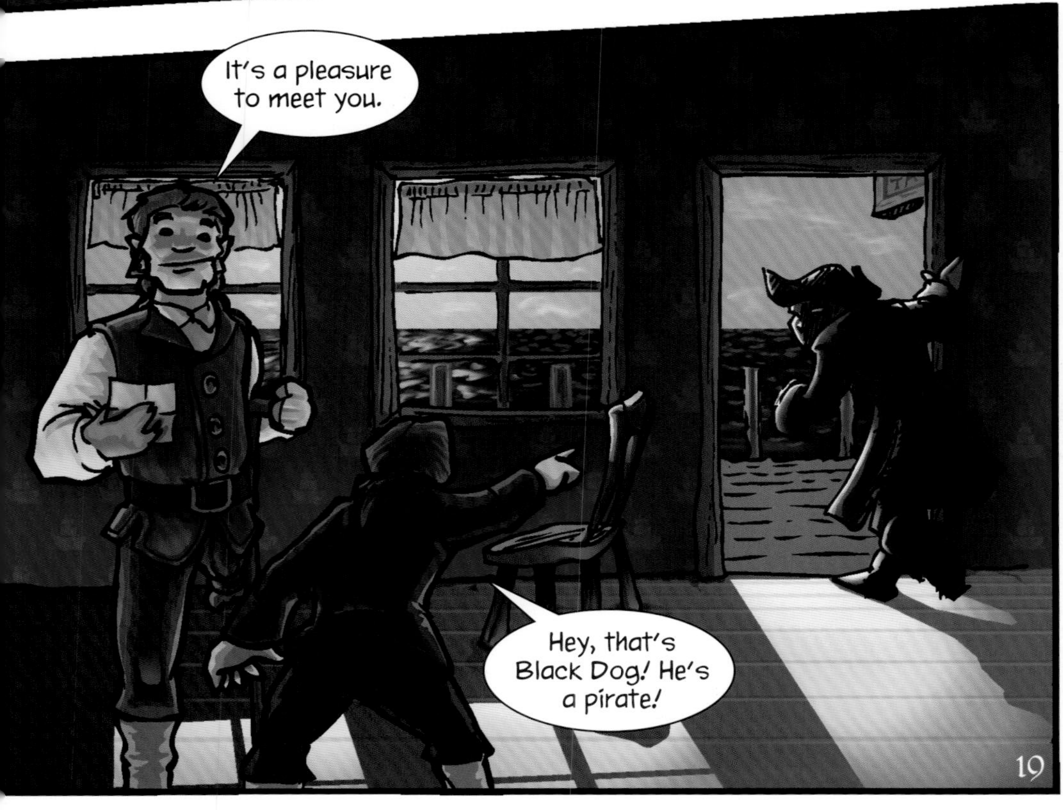
It's a pleasure to meet you.
Hey, that's Black Dog! He's a pirate!

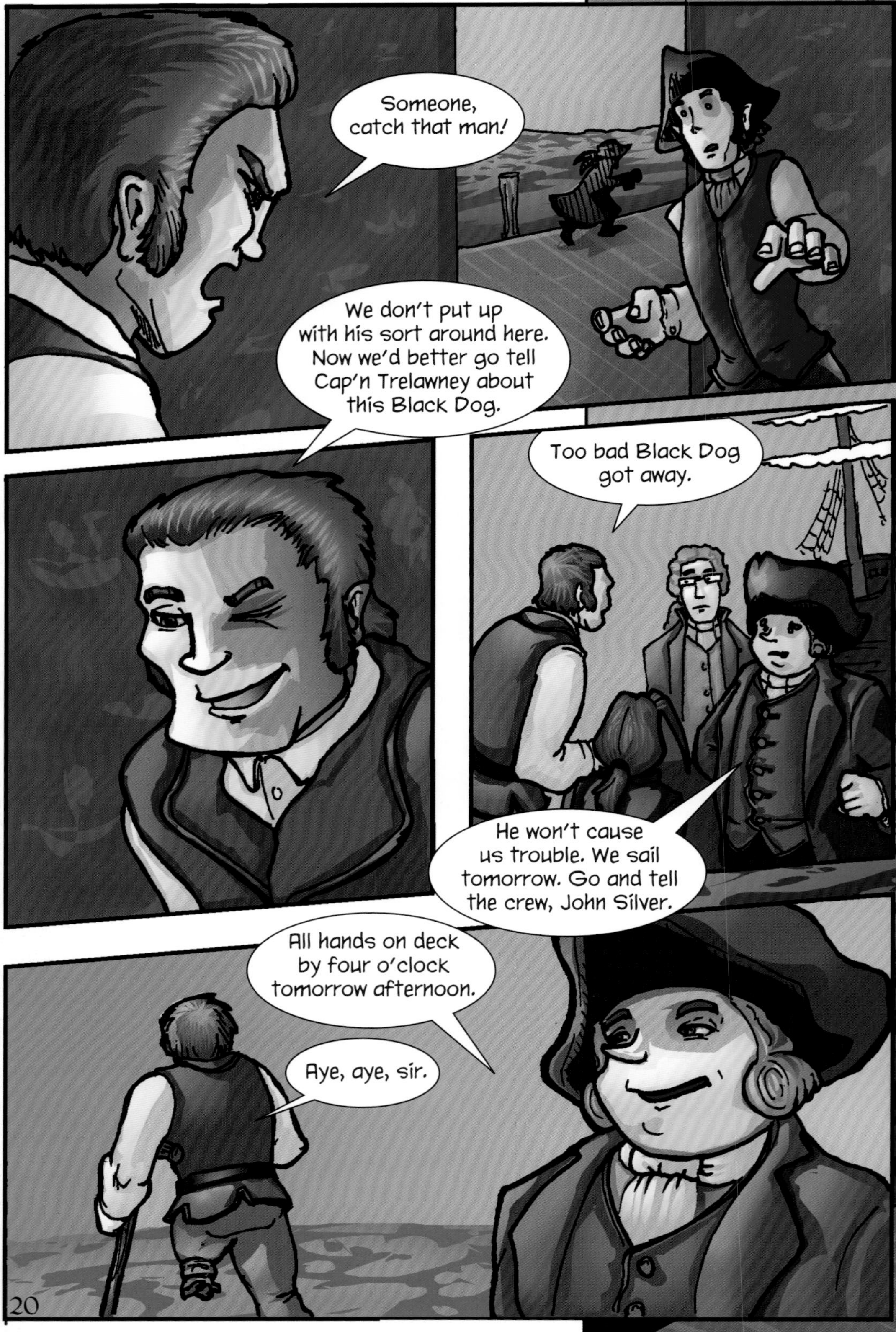
Someone, catch that man!
We don't put up with his sort around here. Now we'd better go tell Cap'n Trelawney about this Black Dog.
Too bad Black Dog got away.
He won't cause us trouble. We sail tomorrow. Go and tell the crew, John Silver.
All hands on deck by four o'clock tomorrow afternoon.
Aye, aye, sir.

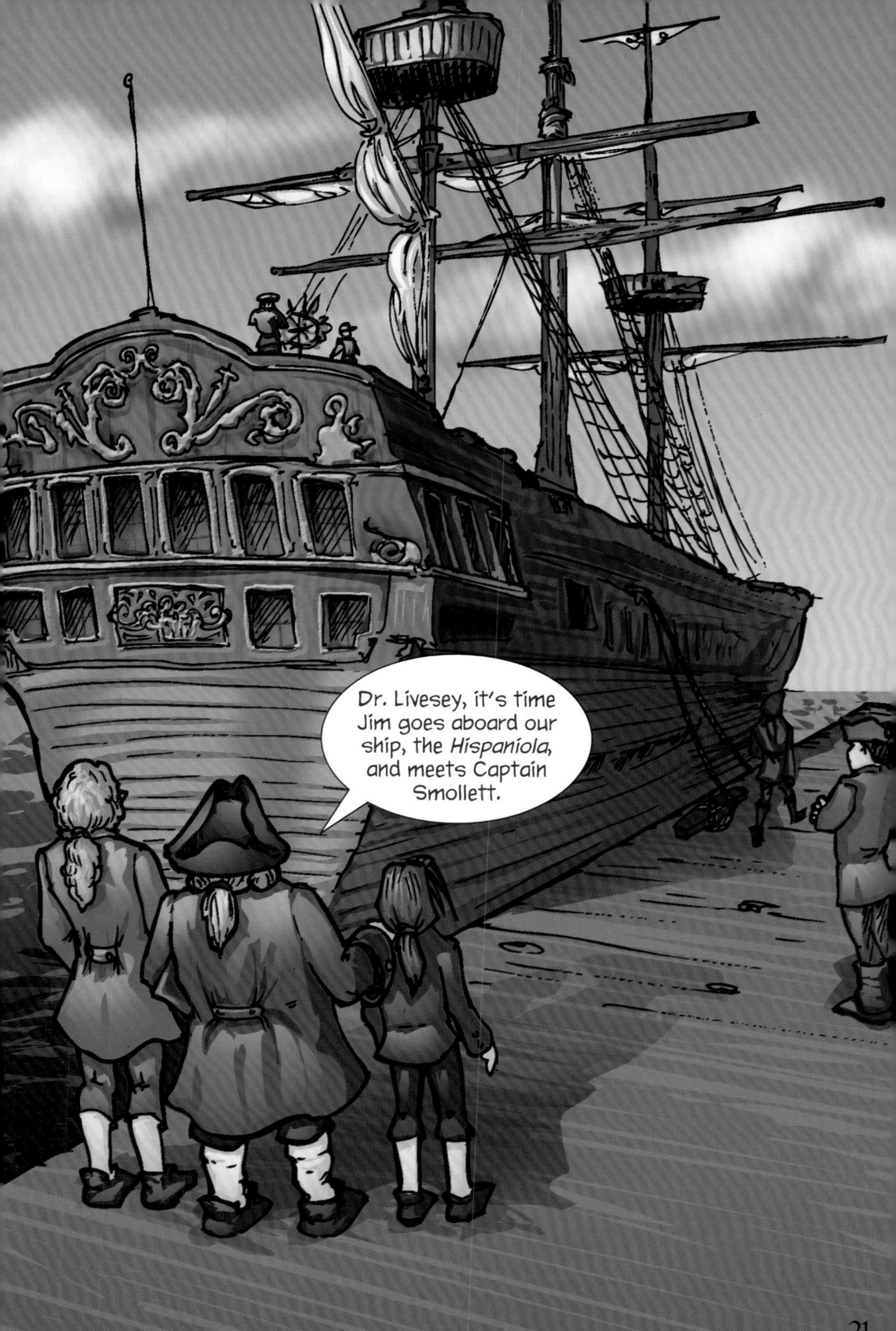
Dr. Livesey, it's time Jim goes aboard our ship, the *Hispaniola*, and meets Captain Smollett.

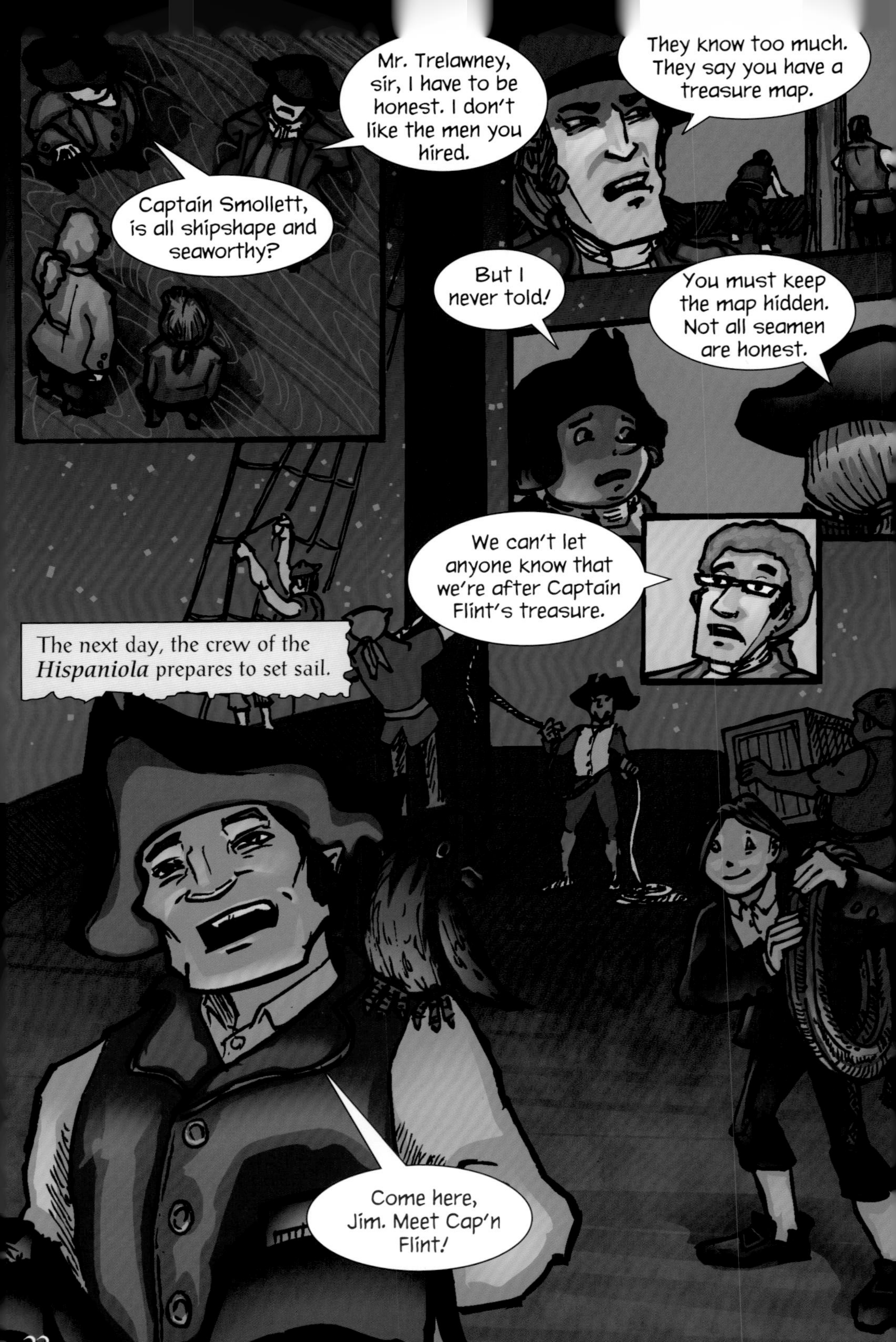
Captain Smollett, is all shipshape and seaworthy?
Mr. Trelawney, sir, I have to be honest. I don't like the men you hired.
They know too much. They say you have a treasure map.
But I never told!
You must keep the map hidden. Not all seamen are honest.
We can't let anyone know that we're after Captain Flint's treasure.
The next day, the crew of the *Hispaniola* prepares to set sail.
Come here, Jim. Meet Cap'n Flint!

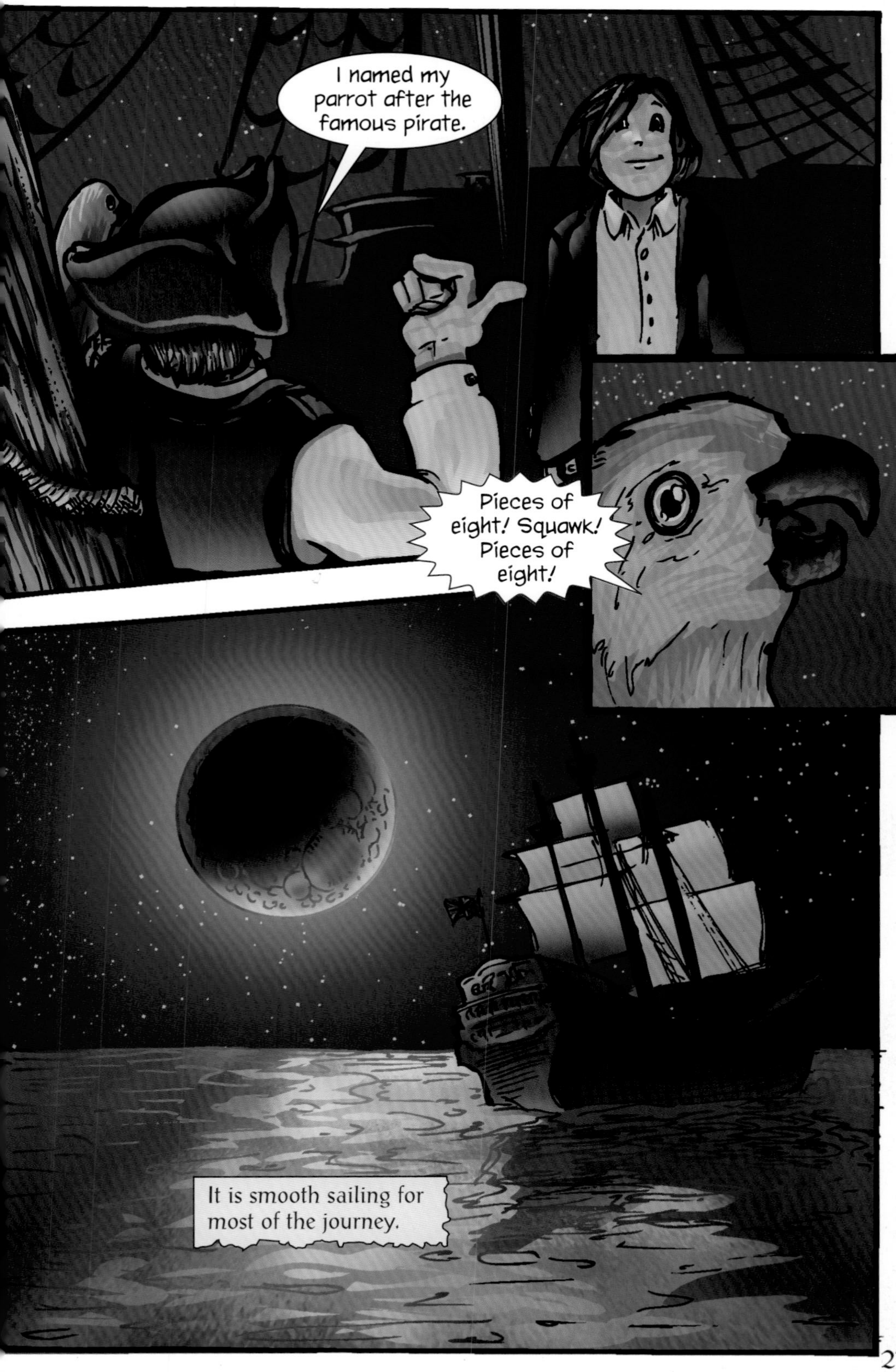
I named my parrot after the famous pirate.
Pieces of eight! Squawk! Pieces of eight!
It is smooth sailing for most of the journey.

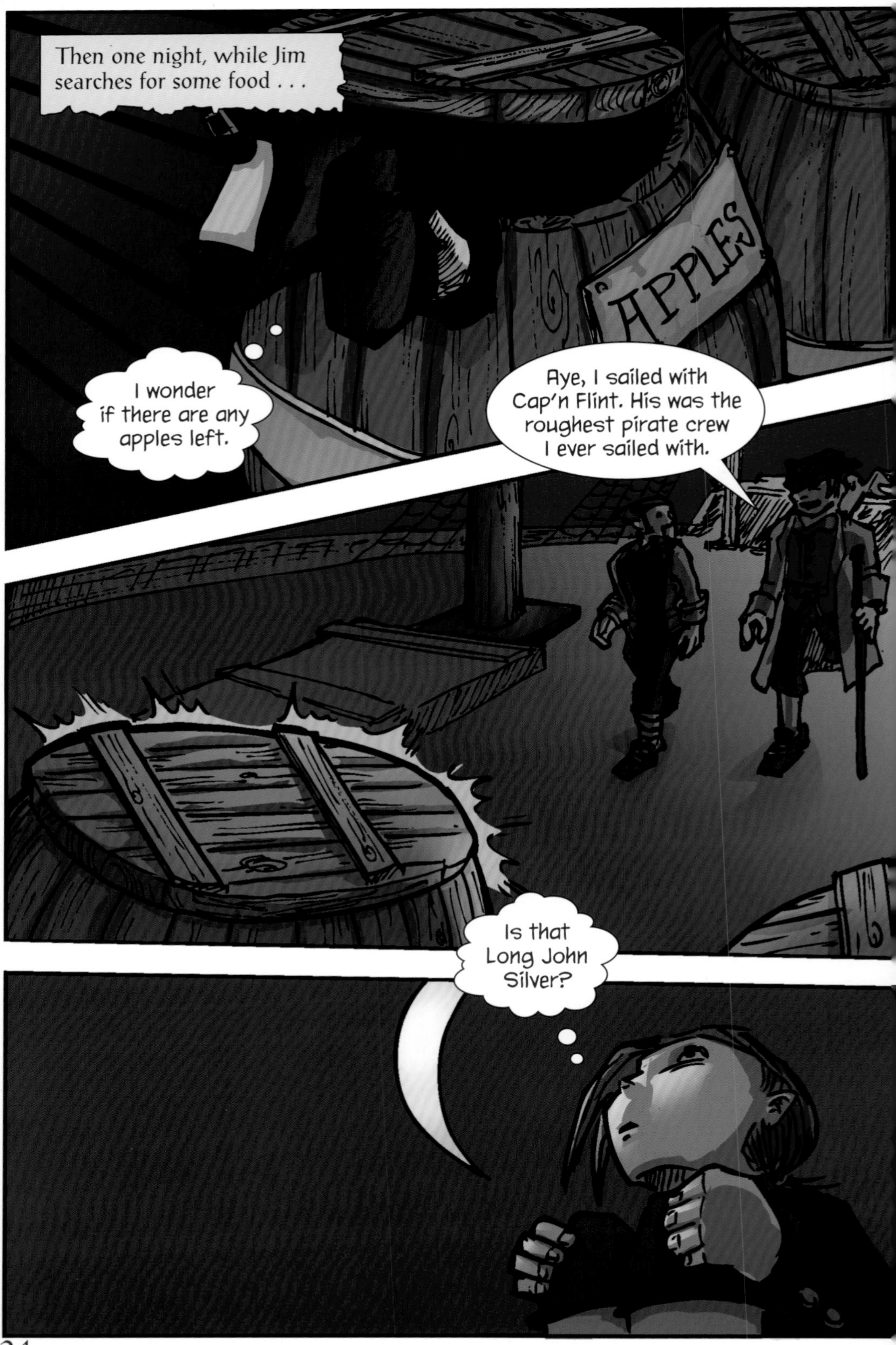
Then one night, while Jim searches for some food . . .
APPLES
I wonder if there are any apples left.
Aye, I sailed with Cap'n Flint. His was the roughest pirate crew I ever sailed with.
Is that Long John Silver?

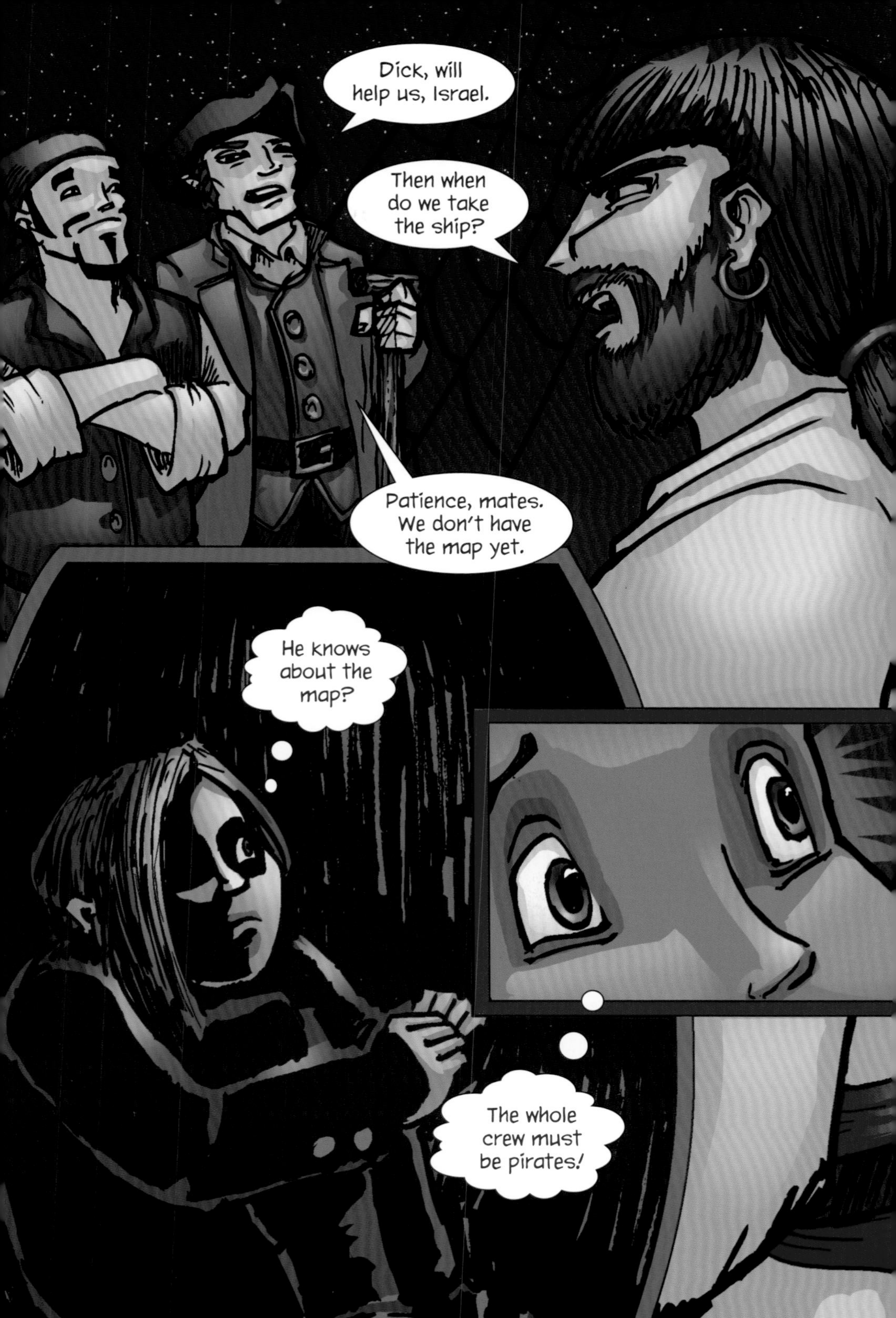
Dick, will help us, Israel.
Then when do we take the ship?
Patience, mates. We don't have the map yet.
He knows about the map?
The whole crew must be pirates!

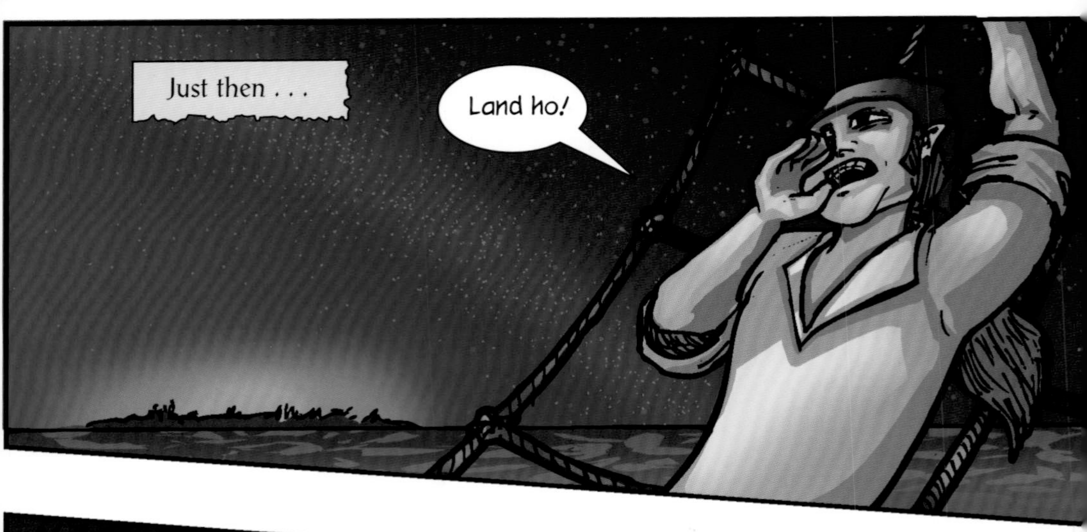
Just then . . .
Land ho!

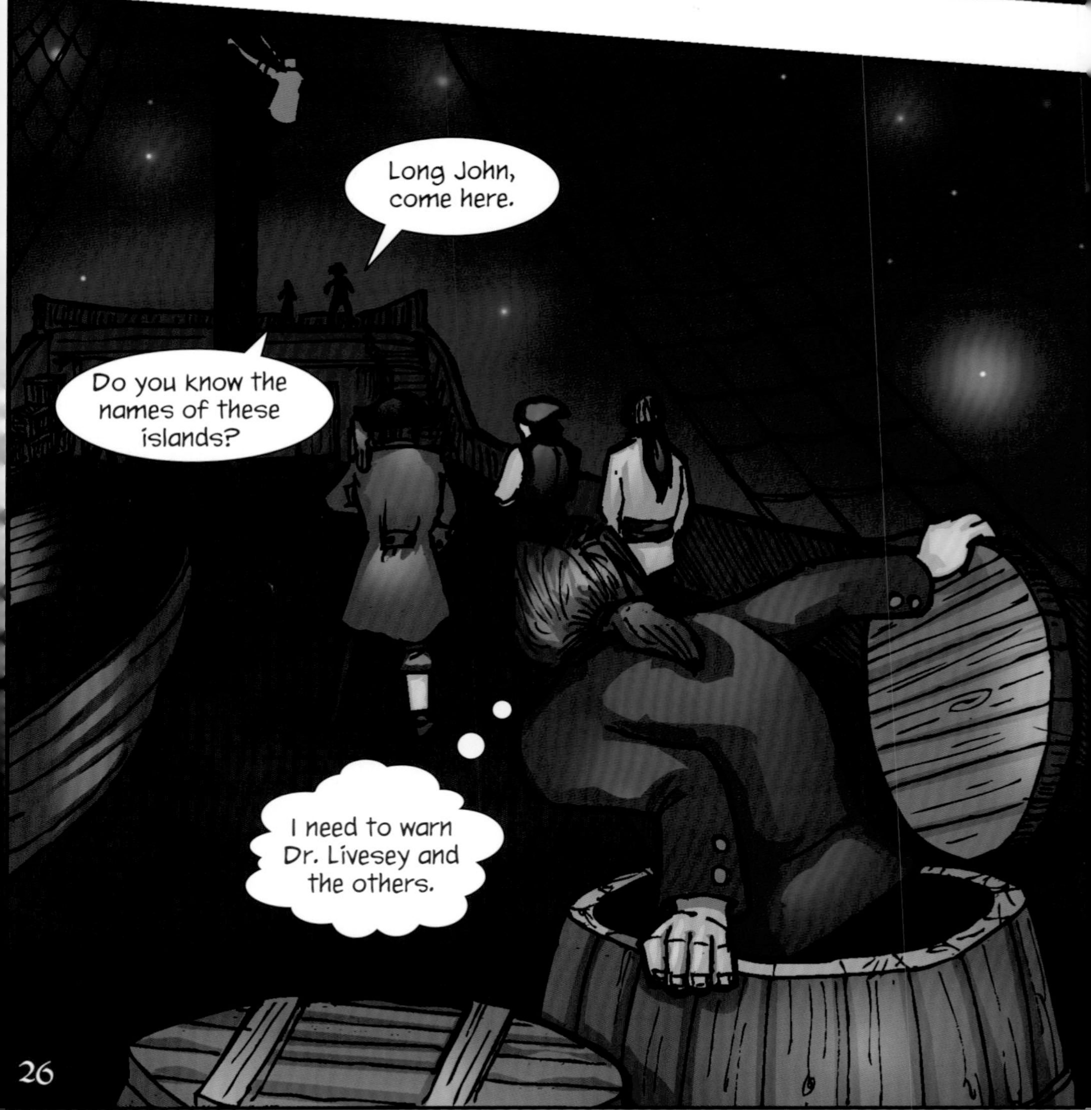
Long John, come here.
Do you know the names of these islands?
I need to warn Dr. Livesey and the others.

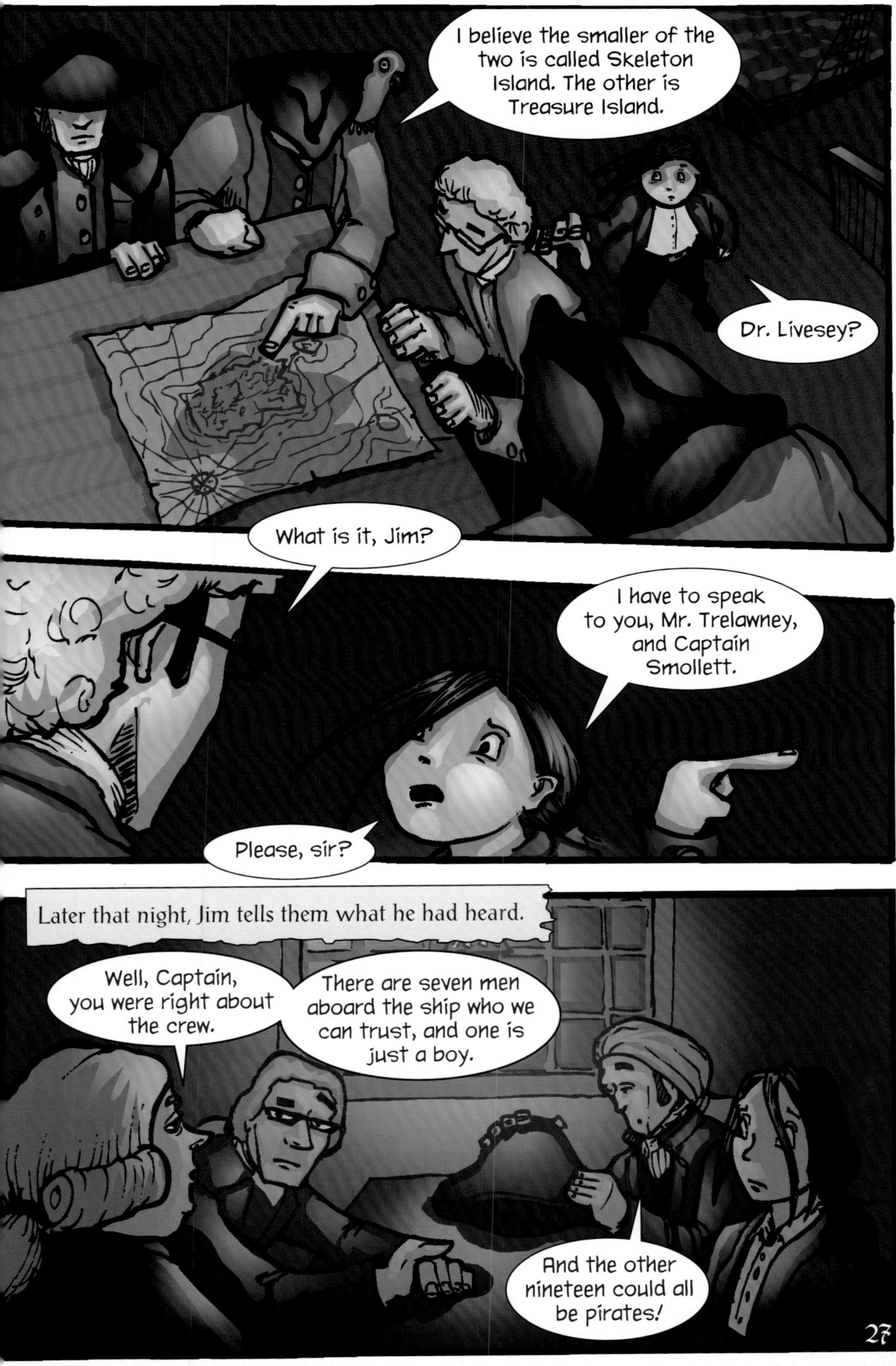
I believe the smaller of the two is called Skeleton Island. The other is Treasure Island.
Dr. Livesey?
What is it, Jim?
Please, sir?
I have to speak to you, Mr. Trelawney, and Captain Smollett.
Later that night, Jim tells them what he had heard.
Well, Captain, you were right about the crew.
There are seven men aboard the ship who we can trust, and one is just a boy.
And the other nineteen could all be pirates!

CHAPTER 3 On the Island

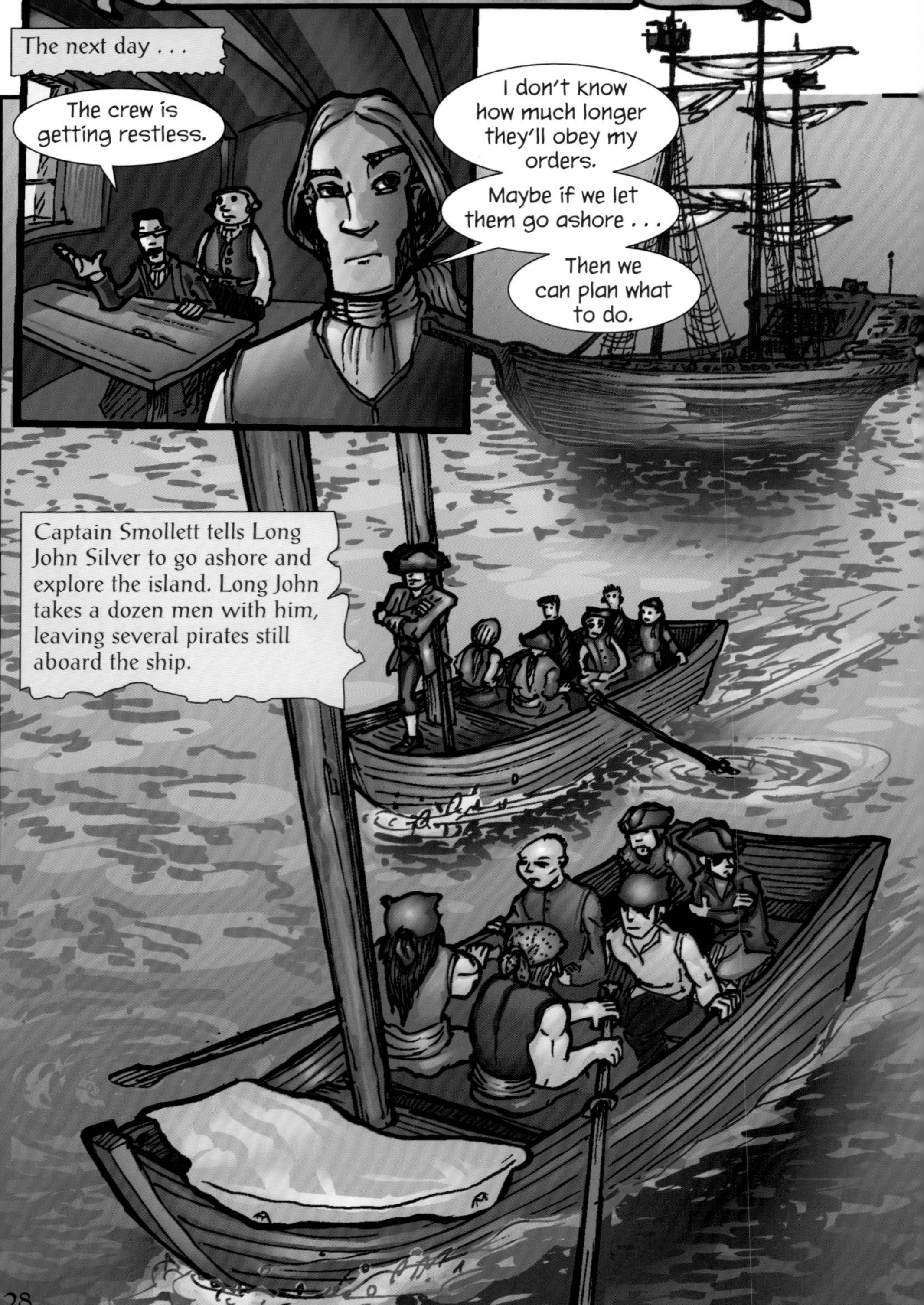
The next day . . .
The crew is getting restless.
I don't know how much longer they'll obey my orders.
Maybe if we let them go ashore . . .
Then we can plan what to do.
Captain Smollett tells Long John Silver to go ashore and explore the island. Long John takes a dozen men with him, leaving several pirates still aboard the ship.

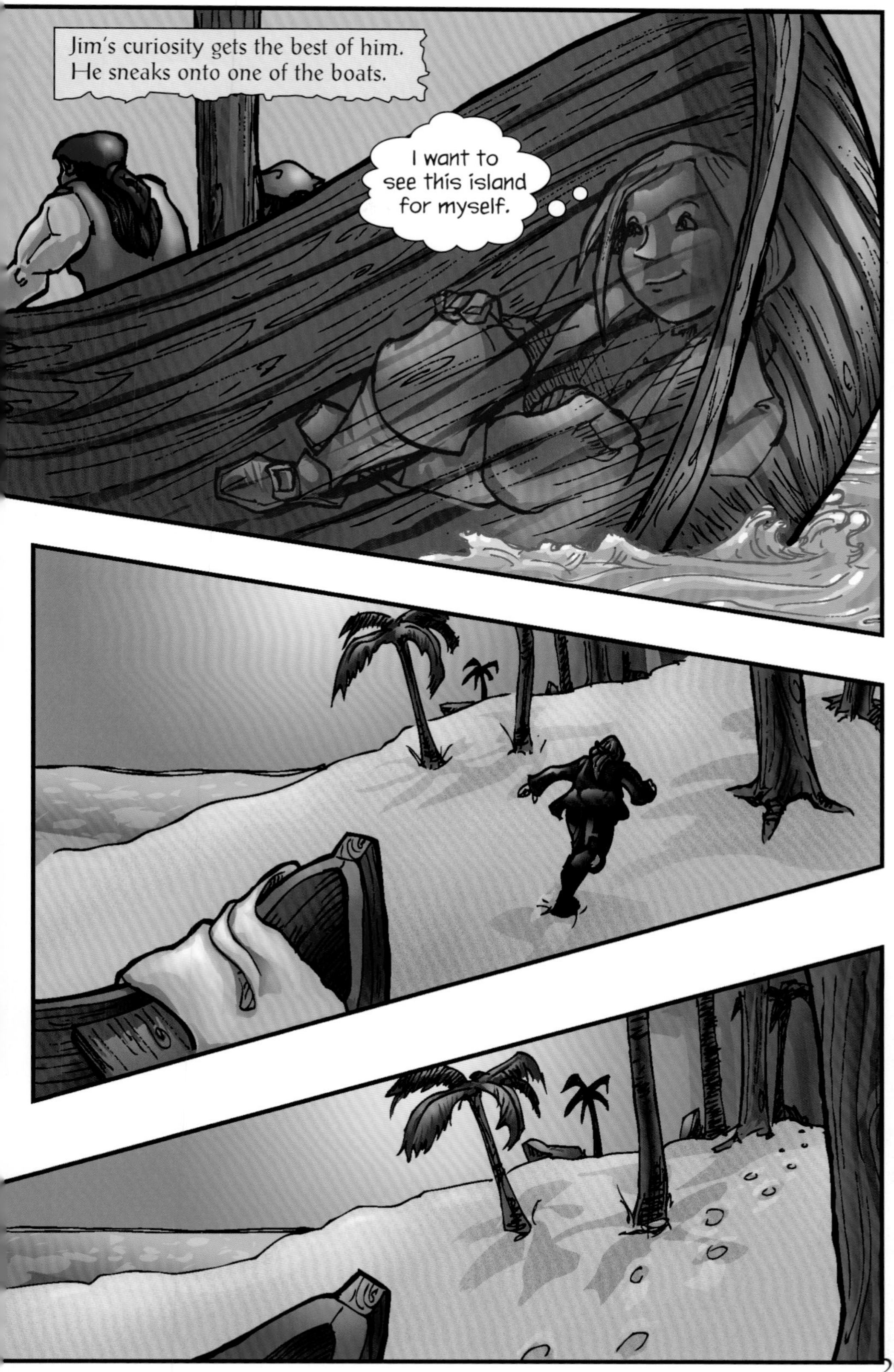
Jim's curiosity gets the best of him. He sneaks onto one of the boats.
I want to see this island for myself.

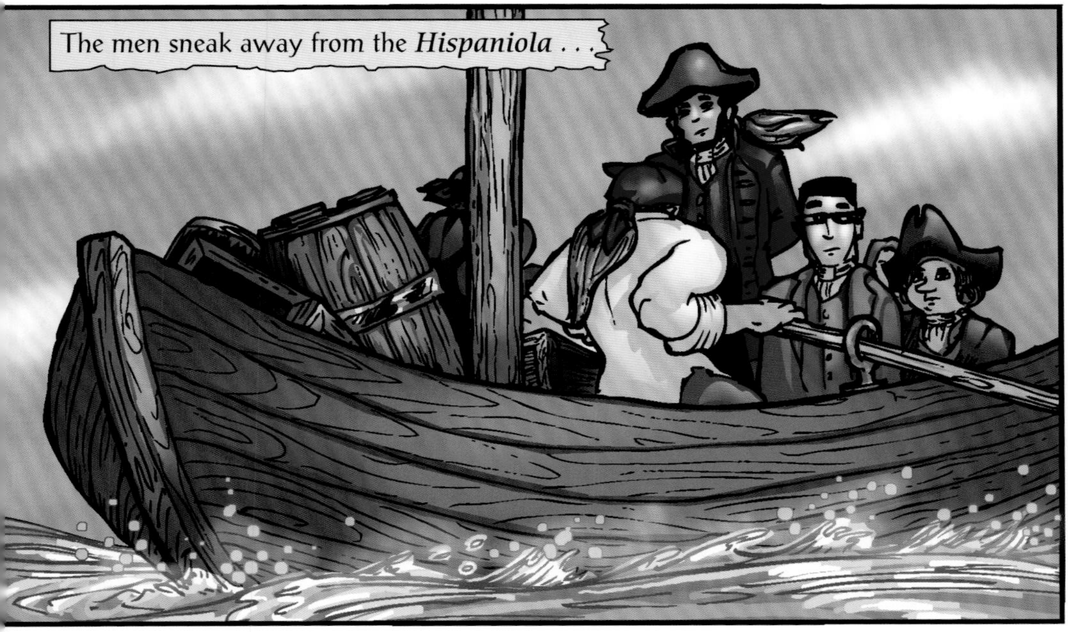
The men sneak away from the *Hispaniola* . . .

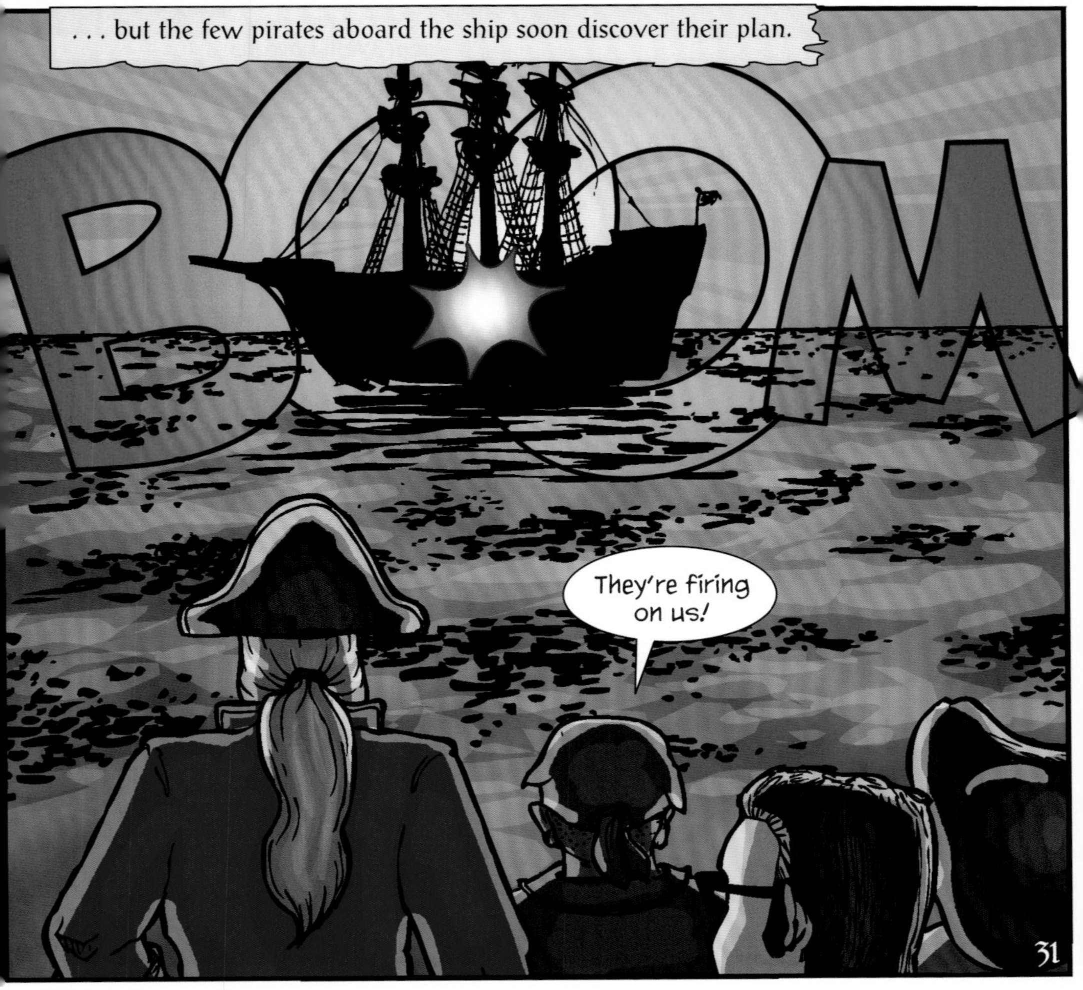
. . . but the few pirates aboard the ship soon discover their plan.
BOOM
They're firing on us!

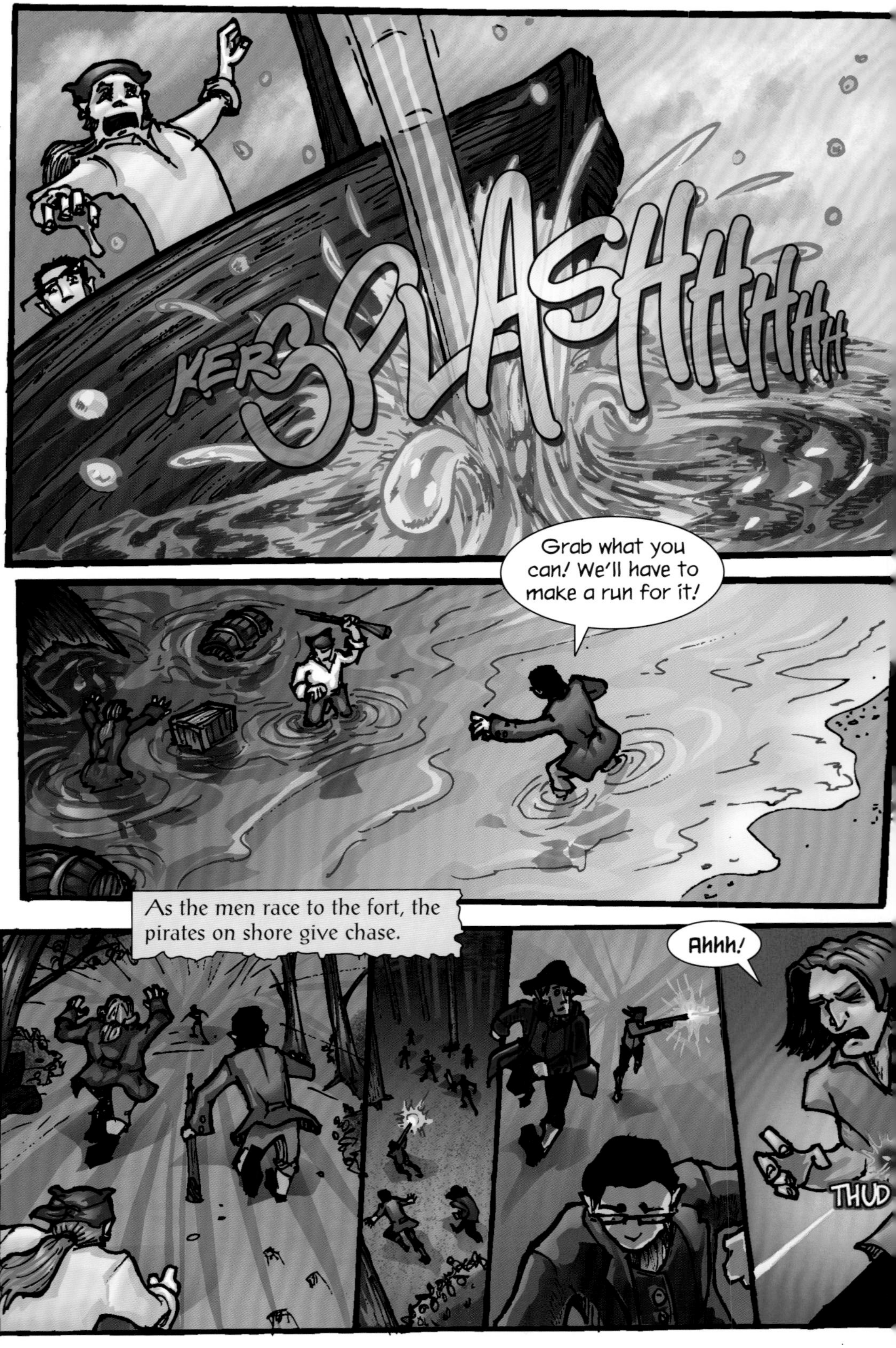

KERSPLASHHHHHH
Grab what you can! We'll have to make a run for it!
As the men race to the fort, the pirates on shore give chase.
Ahhh!
THUD

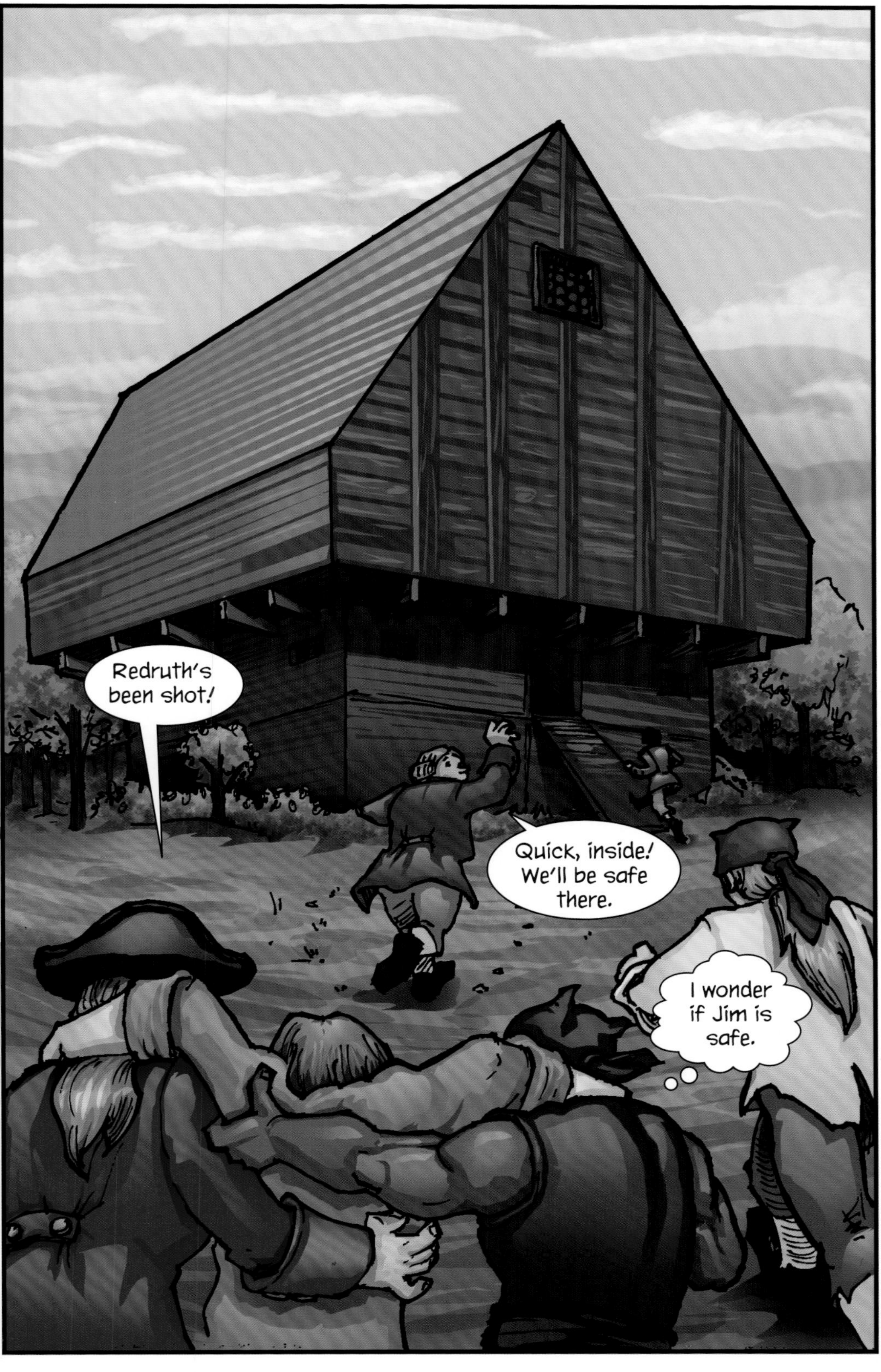
Redruth's been shot!
Quick, inside! We'll be safe there.
I wonder if Jim is safe.

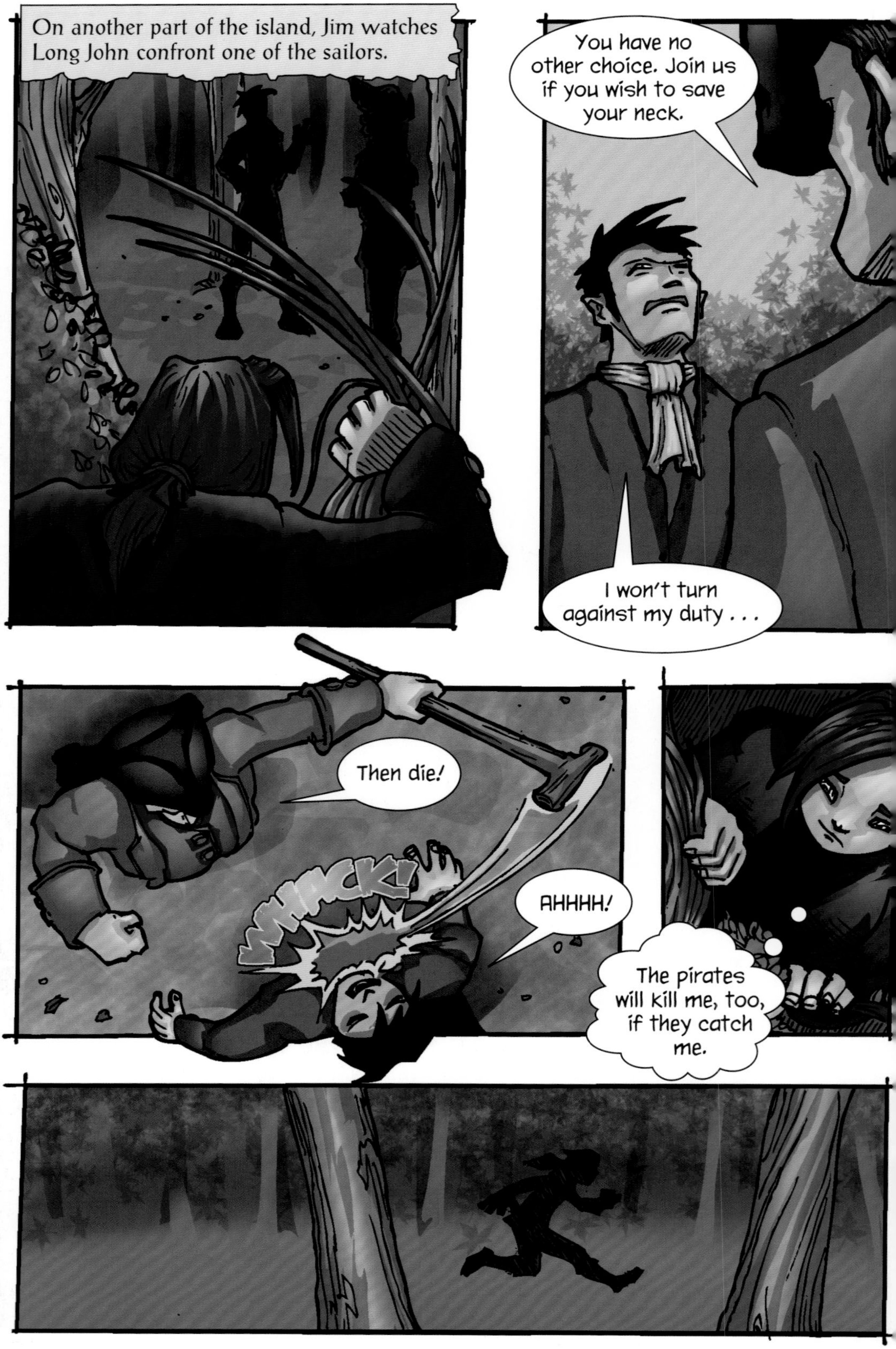
On another part of the island, Jim watches Long John confront one of the sailors.
You have no other choice. Join us if you wish to save your neck.
I won't turn against my duty . . .
Then die!
WHACK!
AHHHH!
The pirates will kill me, too, if they catch me.

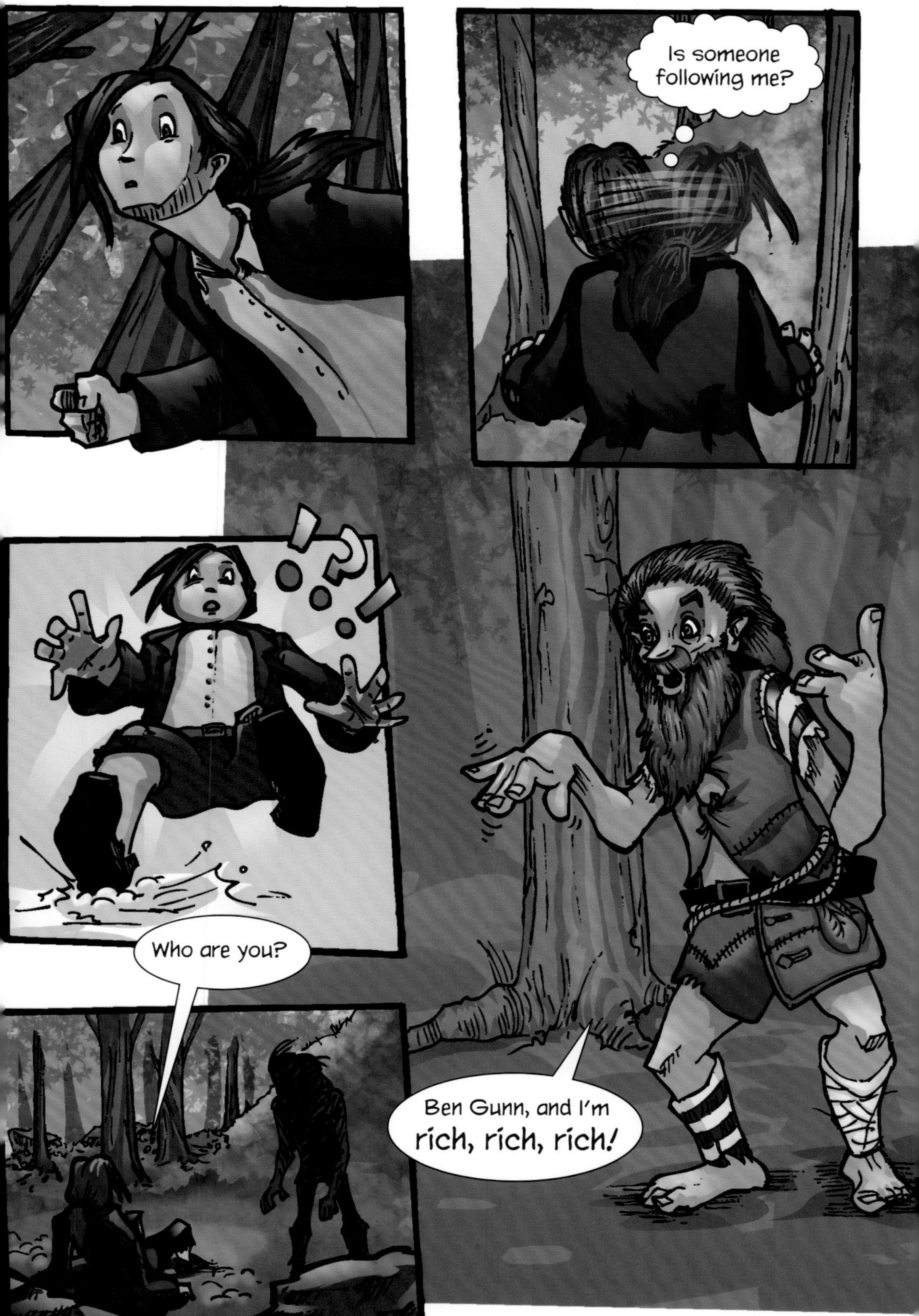
Is someone following me?
Who are you?
Ben Gunn, and I'm rich, rich, rich!

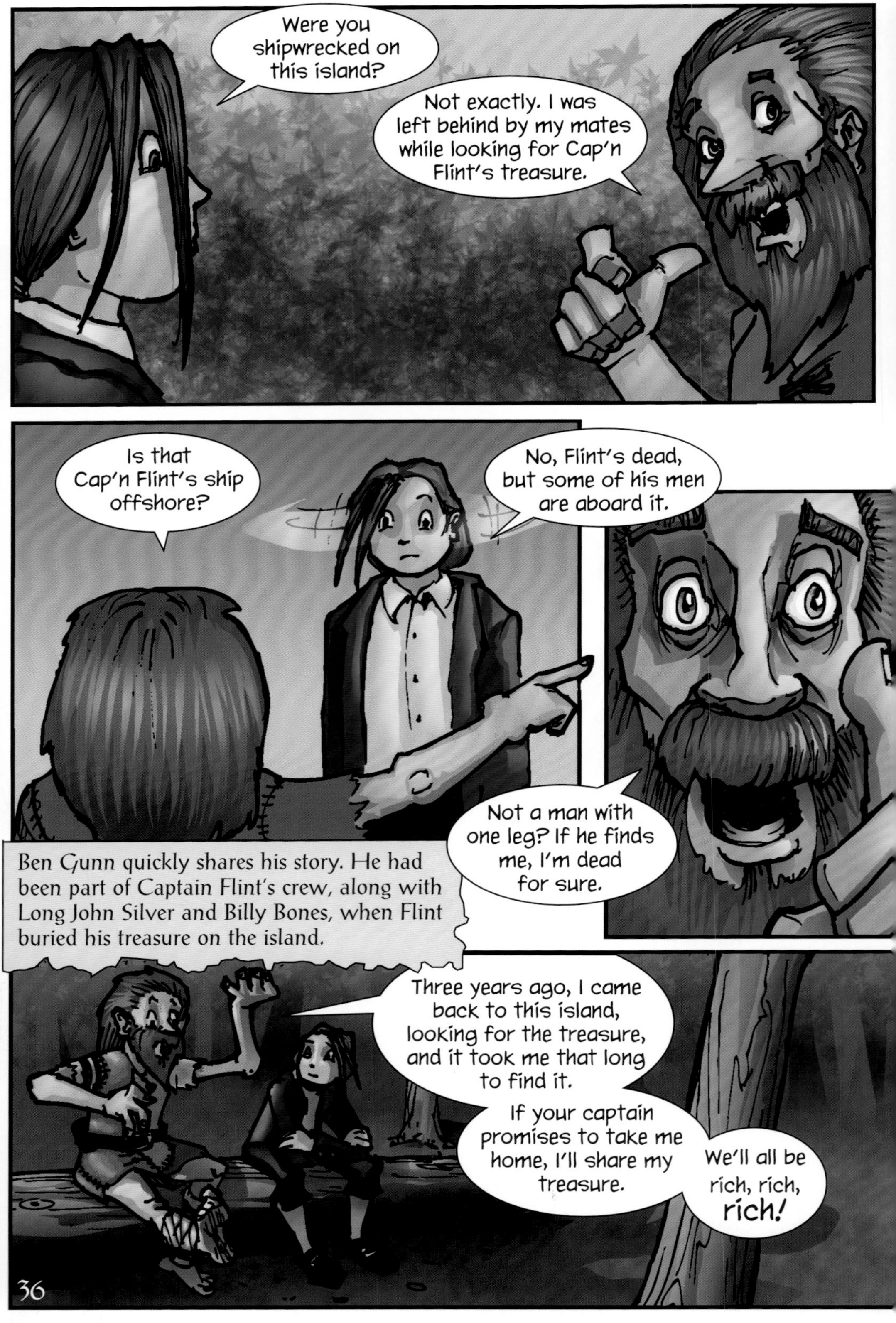
Were you shipwrecked on this island?
Not exactly. I was left behind by my mates while looking for Cap'n Flint's treasure.
Is that Cap'n Flint's ship offshore?
No, Flint's dead, but some of his men are aboard it.
Not a man with one leg? If he finds me, I'm dead for sure.
Ben Gunn quickly shares his story. He had been part of Captain Flint's crew, along with Long John Silver and Billy Bones, when Flint buried his treasure on the island.
Three years ago, I came back to this island, looking for the treasure, and it took me that long to find it.
If your captain promises to take me home, I'll share my treasure.
We'll all be rich, rich, rich!

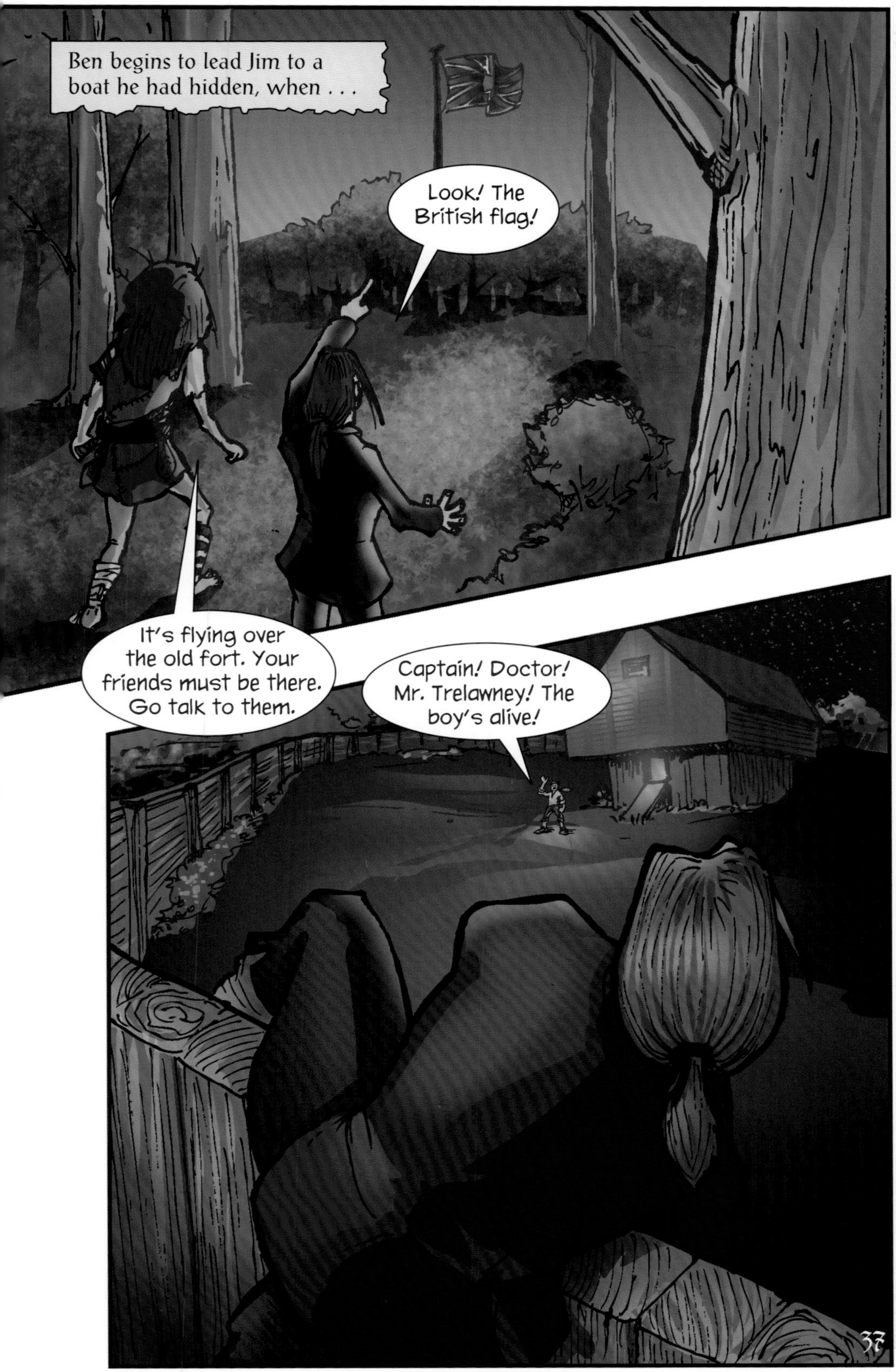
Ben begins to lead Jim to a boat he had hidden, when . . .
Look! The British flag!
It's flying over the old fort. Your friends must be there. Go talk to them.
Captain! Doctor! Mr. Trelawney! The boy's alive!

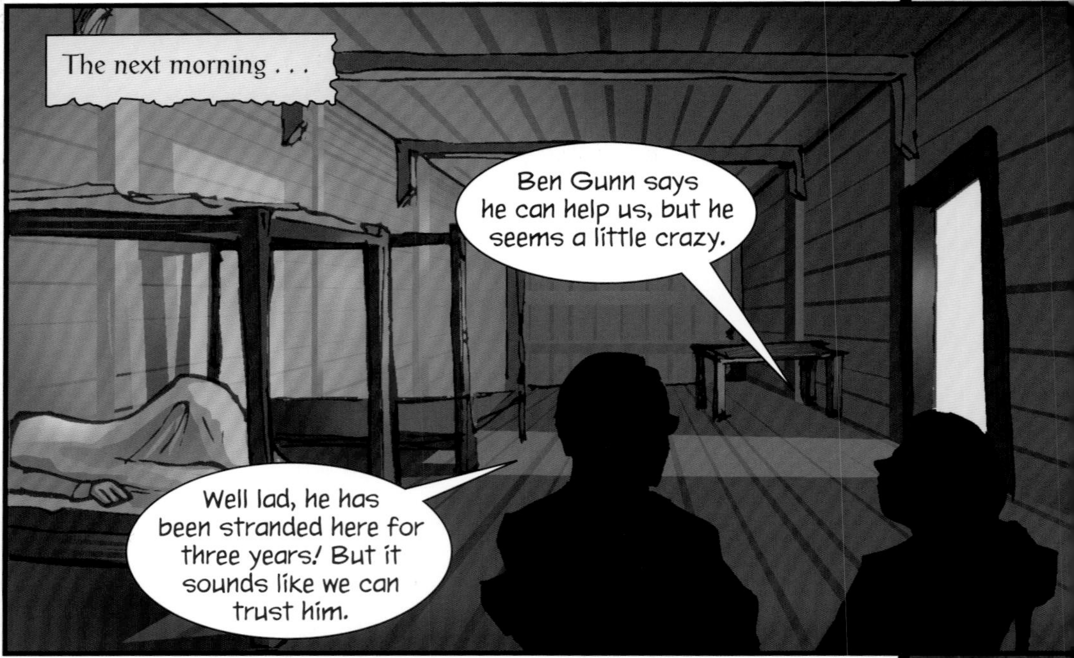
The next morning . . .
Ben Gunn says he can help us, but he seems a little crazy.
Well lad, he has been stranded here for three years! But it sounds like we can trust him.

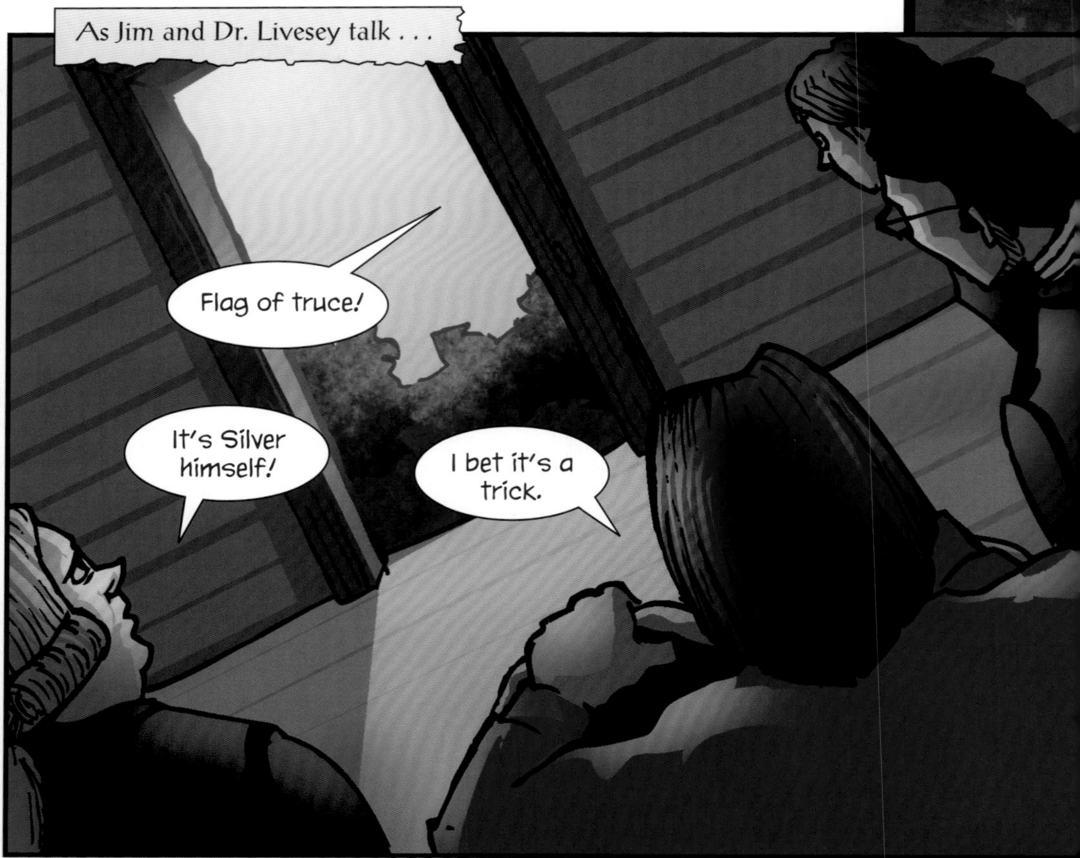
As Jim and Dr. Livesey talk . . .
Flag of truce!
It's Silver himself!
I bet it's a trick.

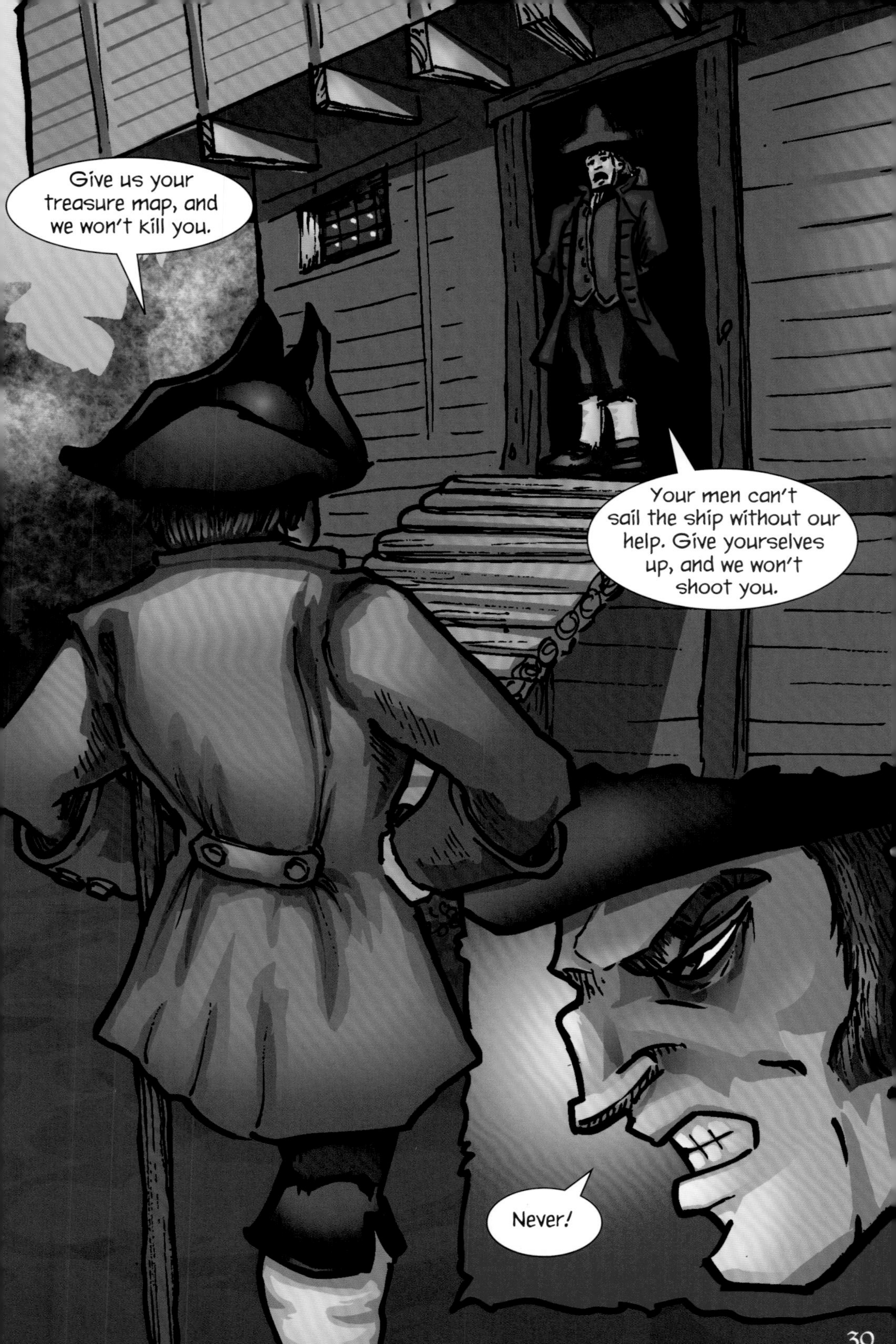
Give us your treasure map, and we won't kill you.
Your men can't sail the ship without our help. Give yourselves up, and we won't shoot you.
Never!

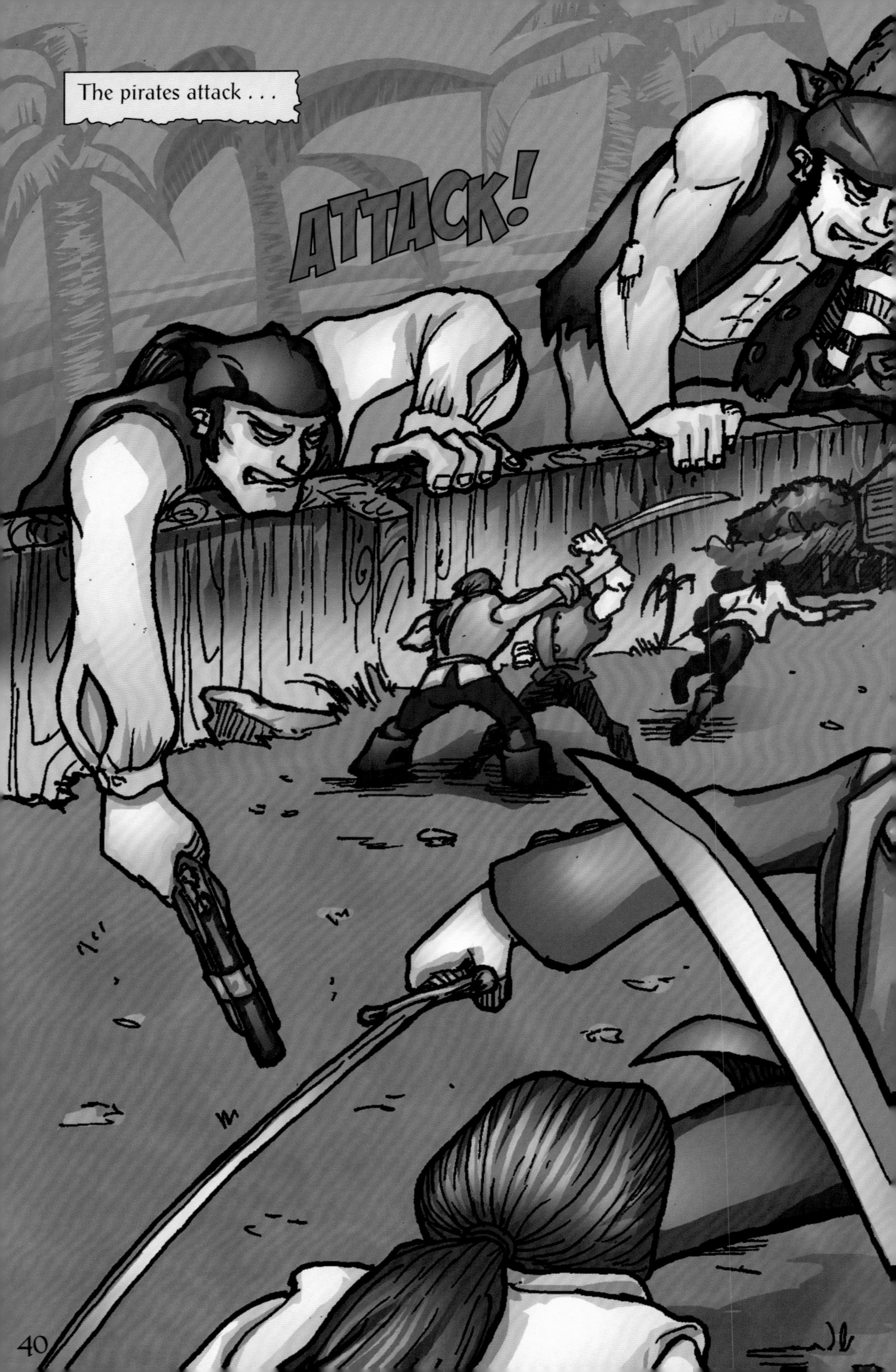
The pirates attack . . .
ATTACK!

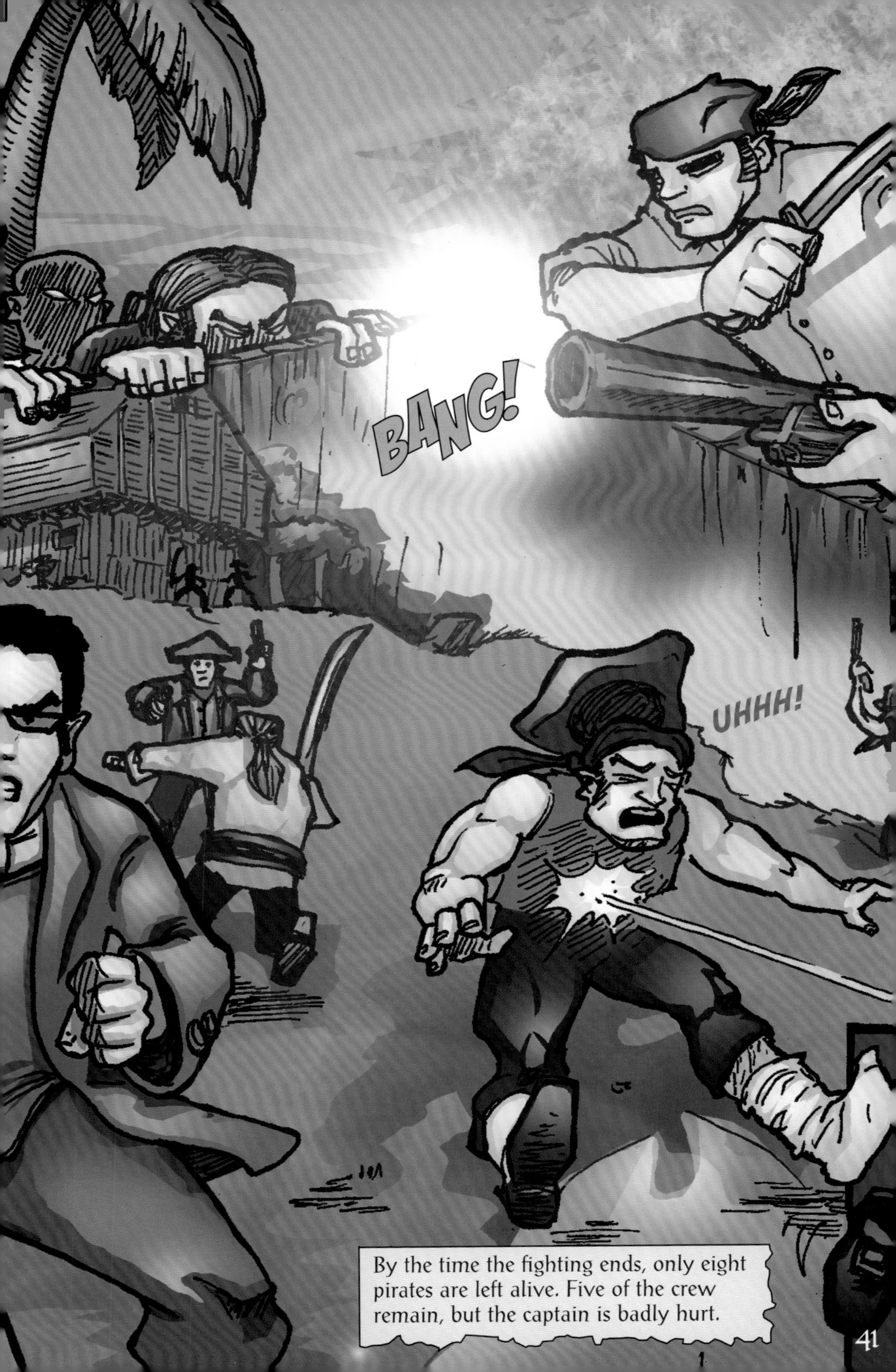
BANG!
UHHH!
By the time the fighting ends, only eight pirates are left alive. Five of the crew remain, but the captain is badly hurt.

CHAPTER 4 Jim's Sea Adventure

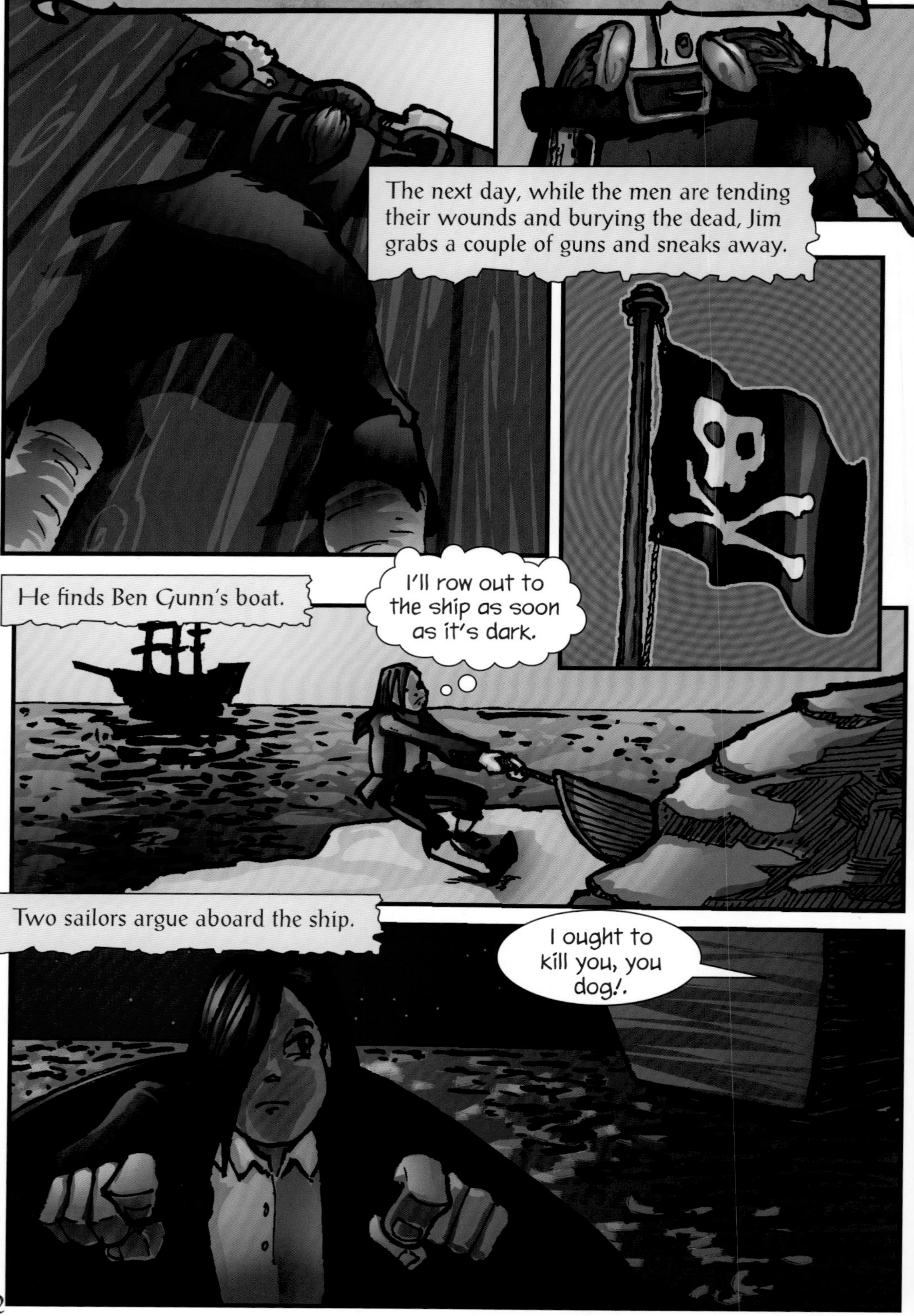
The next day, while the men are tending their wounds and burying the dead, Jim grabs a couple of guns and sneaks away.
He finds Ben Gunn's boat.
I'll row out to the ship as soon as it's dark.
Two sailors argue aboard the ship.
I ought to kill you, you dog!.

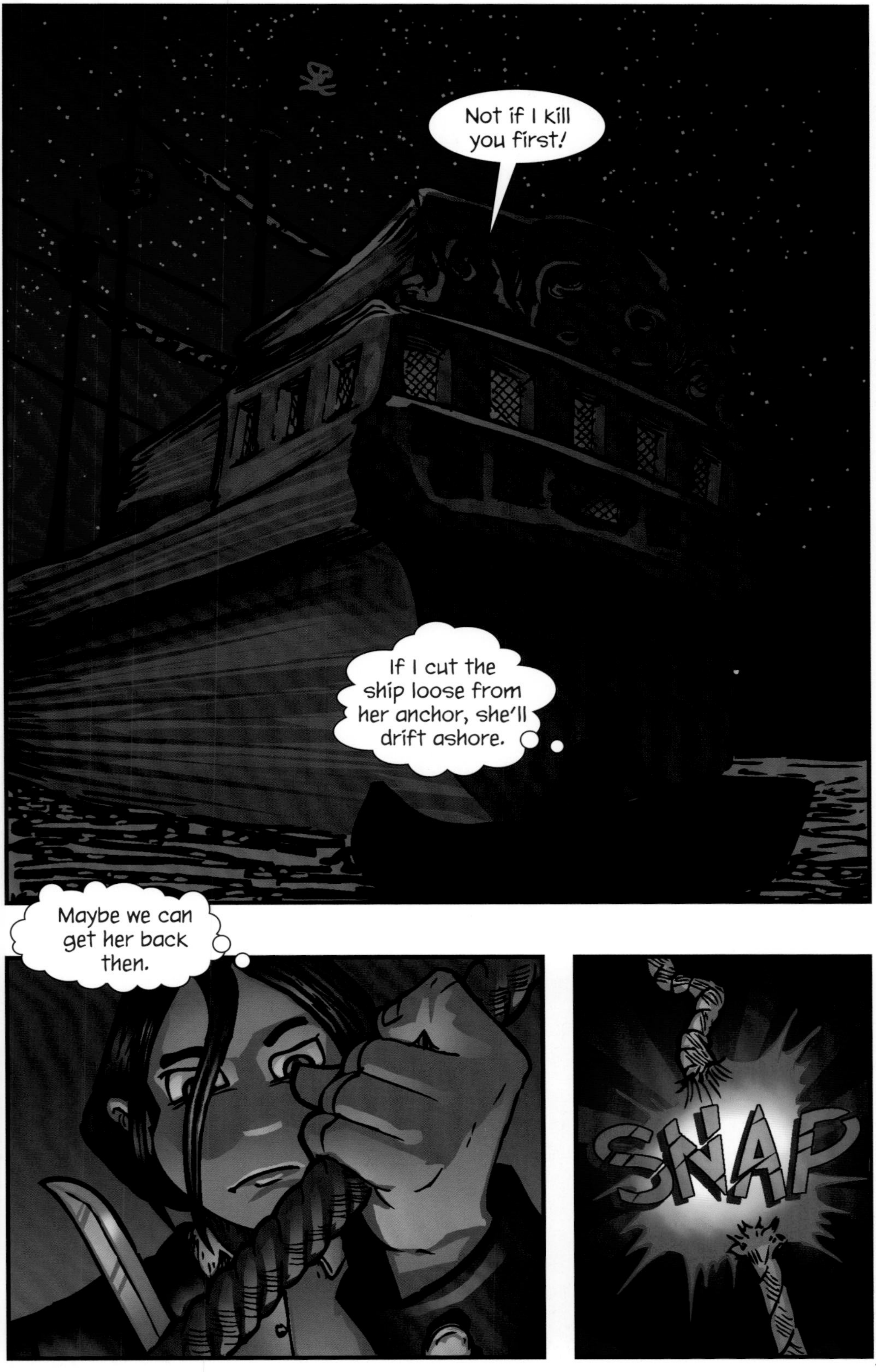
Not if I kill you first!
If I cut the ship loose from her anchor, she'll drift ashore.
Maybe we can get her back then.
SNAP

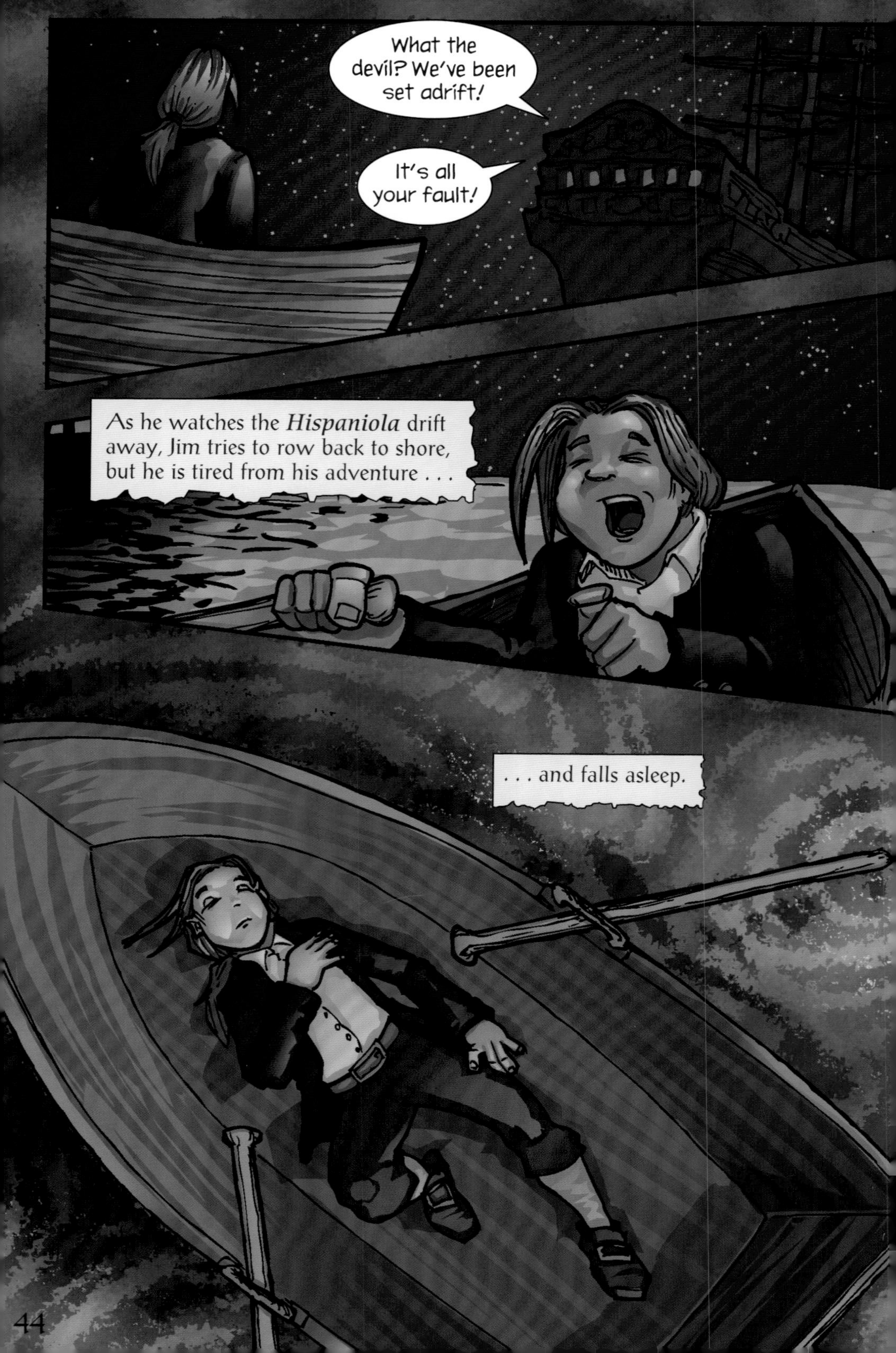
What the devil? We've been set adrift!
It's all your fault!
As he watches the *Hispaniola* drift away, Jim tries to row back to shore, but he is tired from his adventure . . .
. . . and falls asleep.

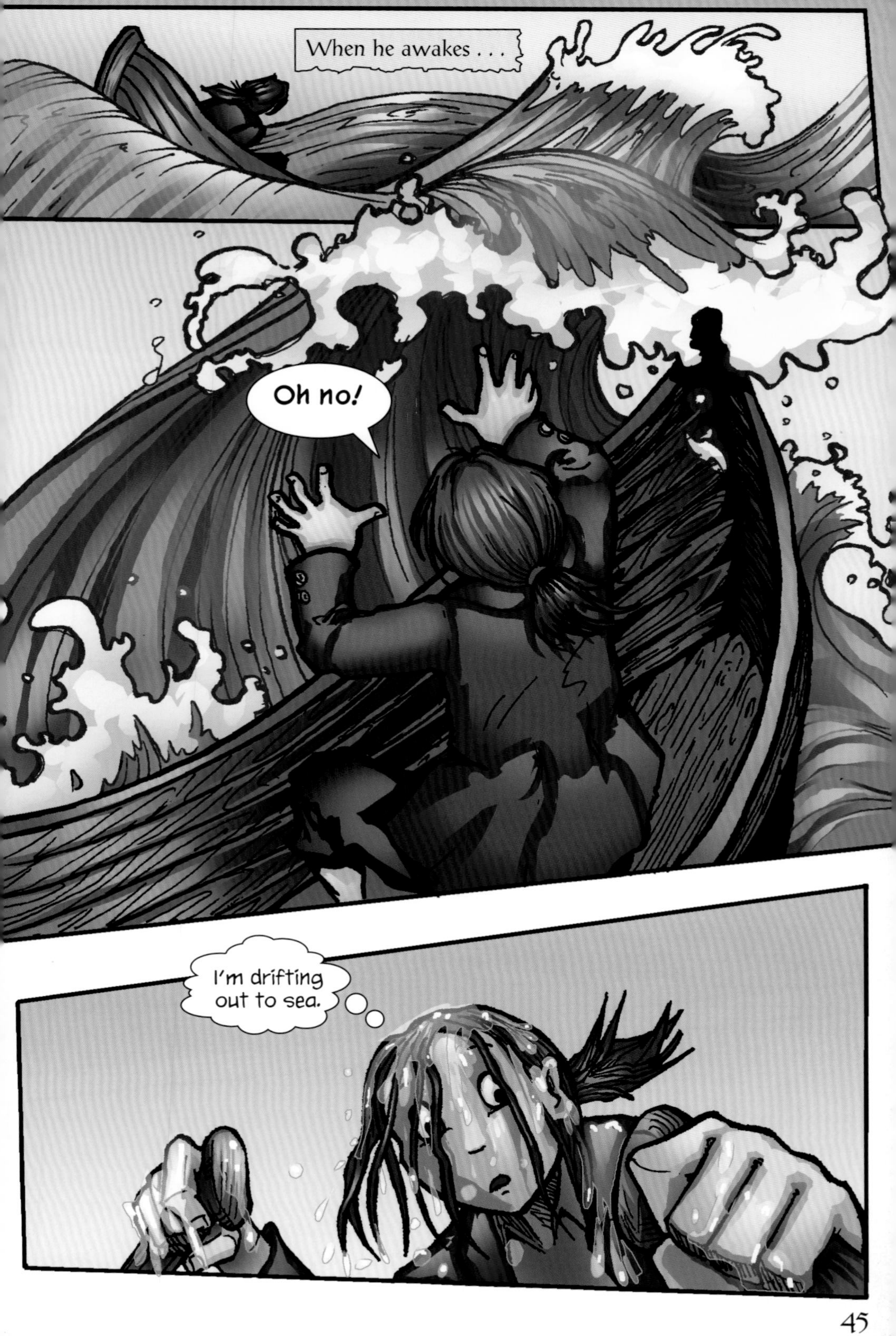
When he awakes . . .
Oh no!
I'm drifting out to sea.

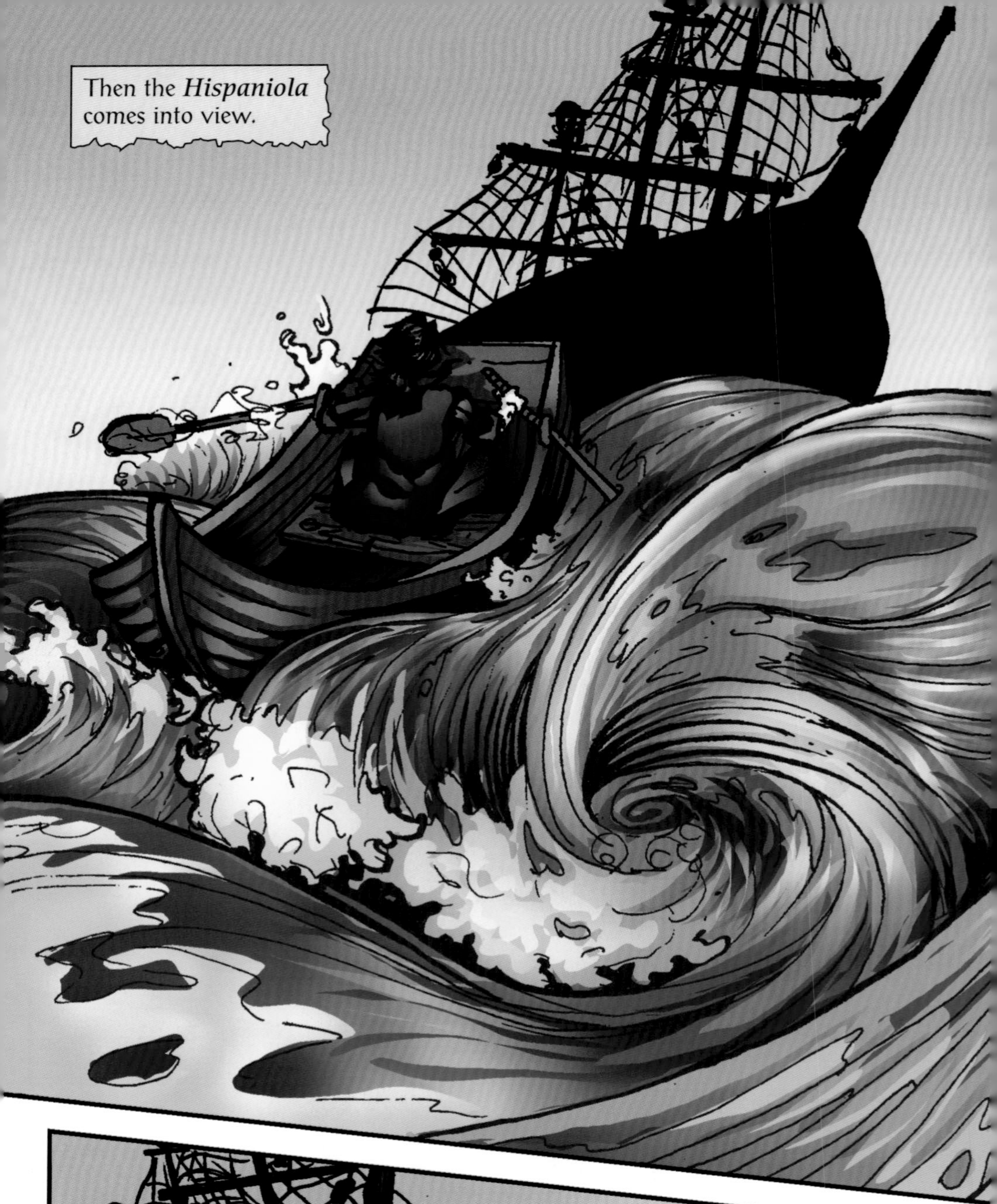
Then the *Hispaniola* comes into view.

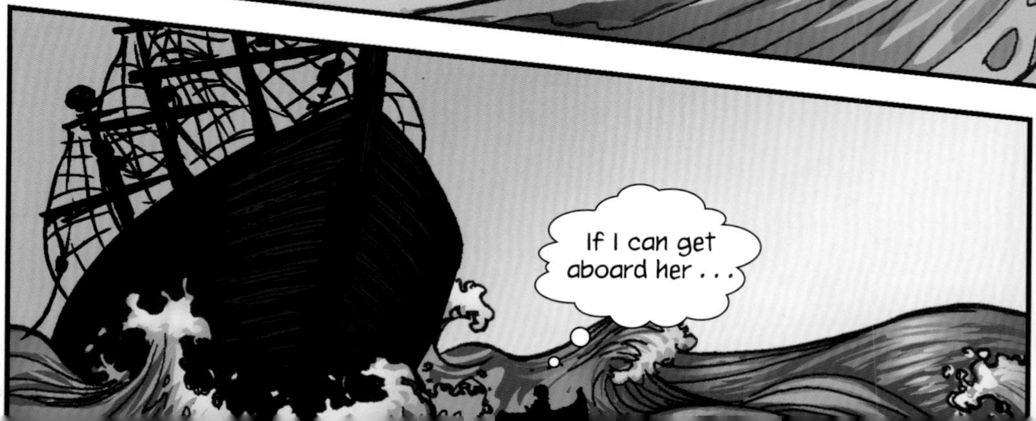
If I can get aboard her . . .

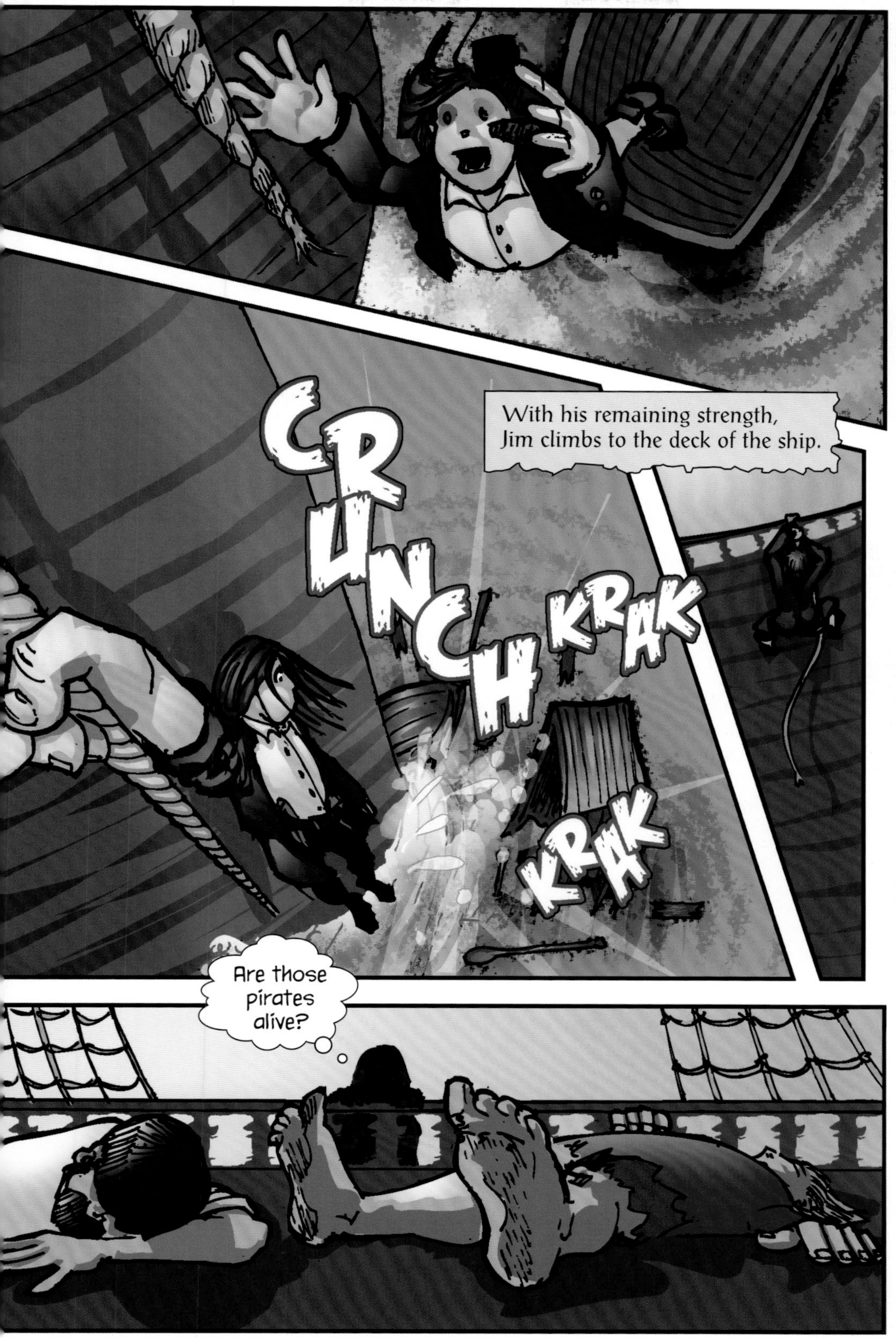
CRUNCH
With his remaining strength, Jim climbs to the deck of the ship.
KRAK
KRAK
Are those pirates alive?

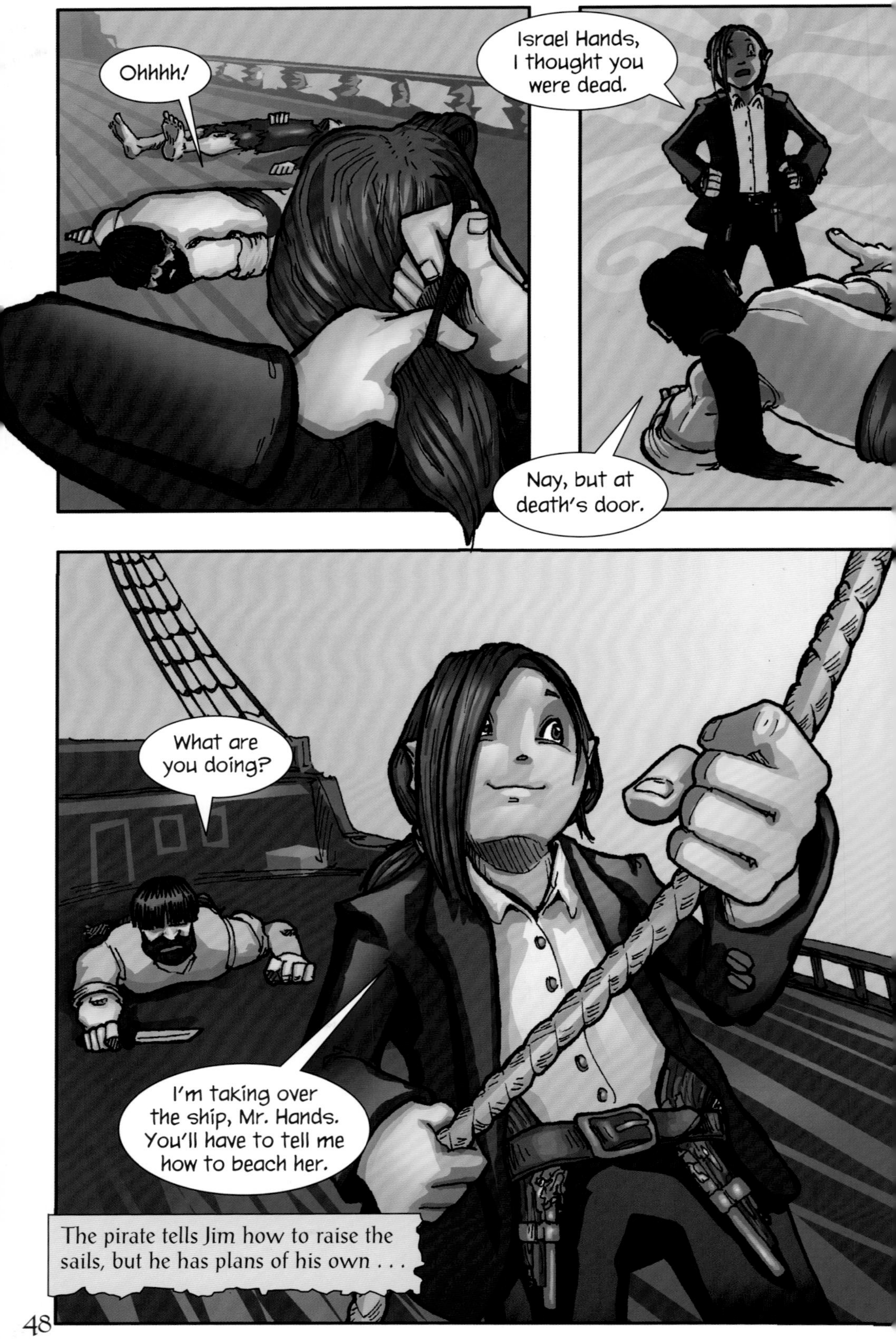

Ohhhh!
Israel Hands, I thought you were dead.
Nay, but at death's door.
What are you doing?
I'm taking over the ship, Mr. Hands. You'll have to tell me how to beach her.
The pirate tells Jim how to raise the sails, but he has plans of his own . . .

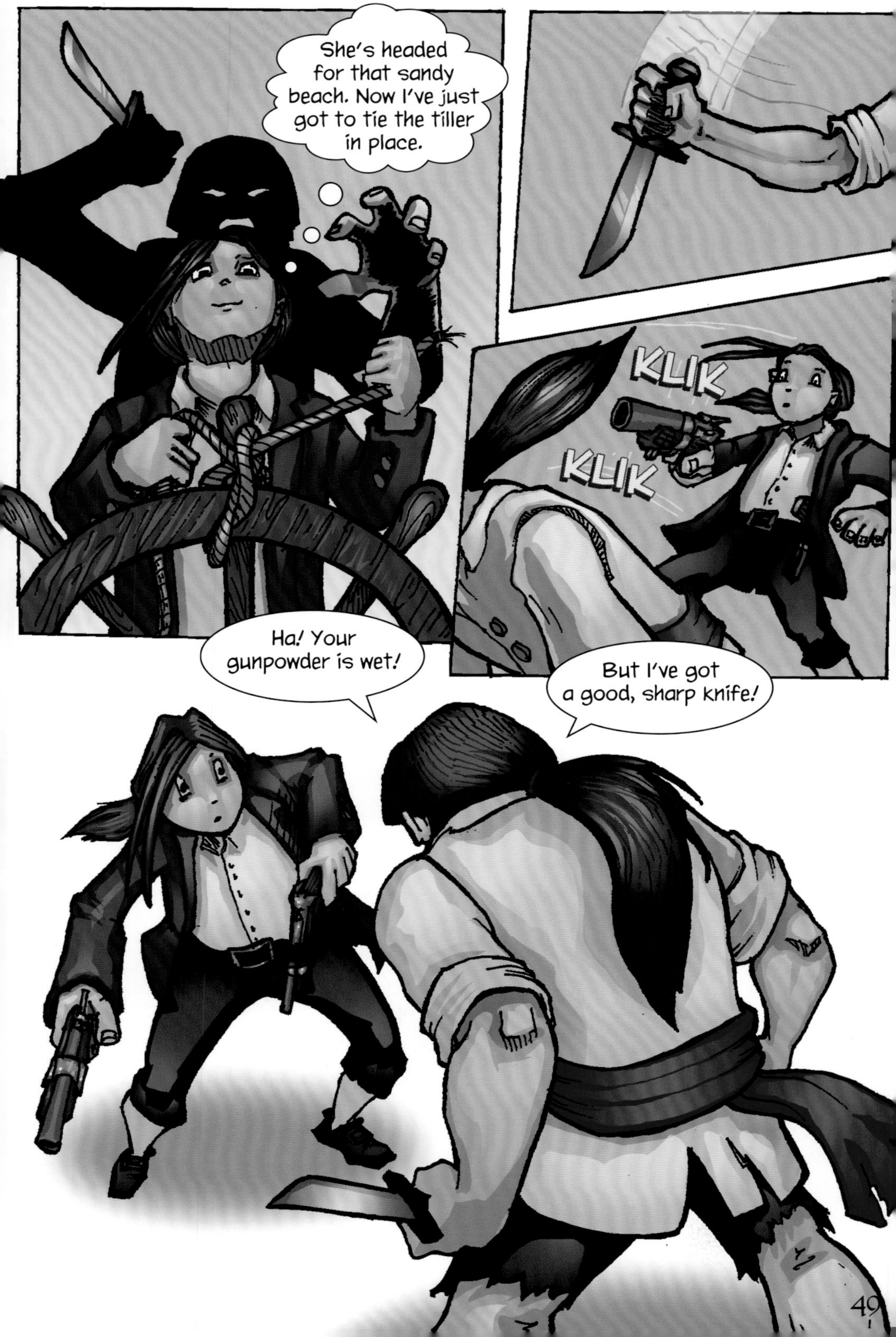
She's headed for that sandy beach. Now I've just got to tie the tiller in place.
KLIK
KLIK
Ha! Your gunpowder is wet!
But I've got a good, sharp knife!

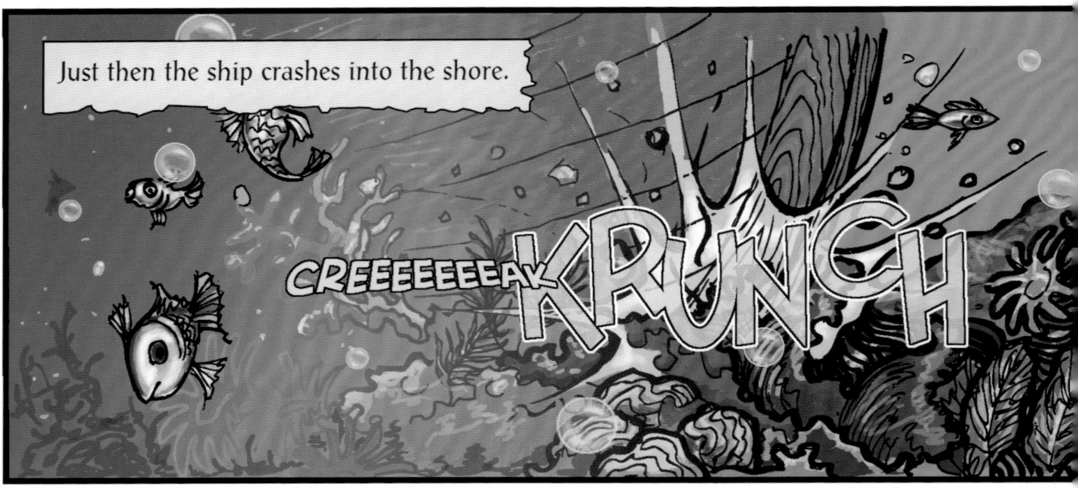
Just then the ship crashes into the shore.
CREEEEEEEAK
KRUNCH

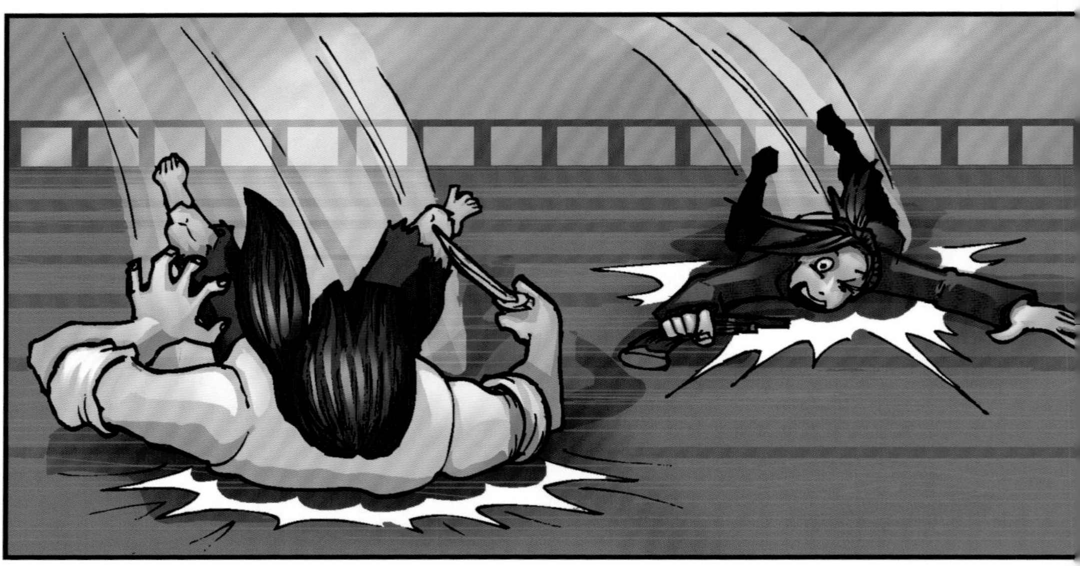

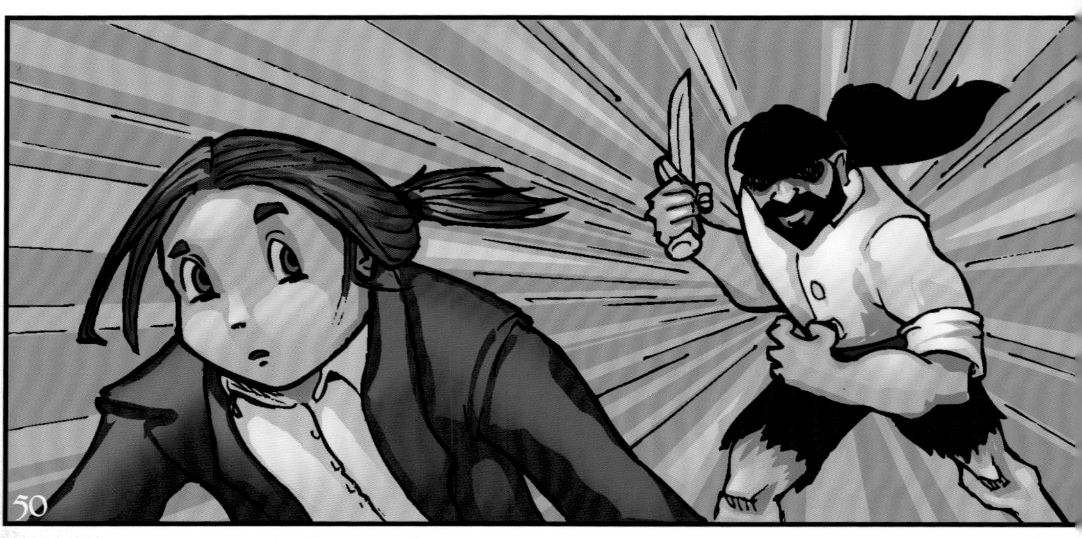

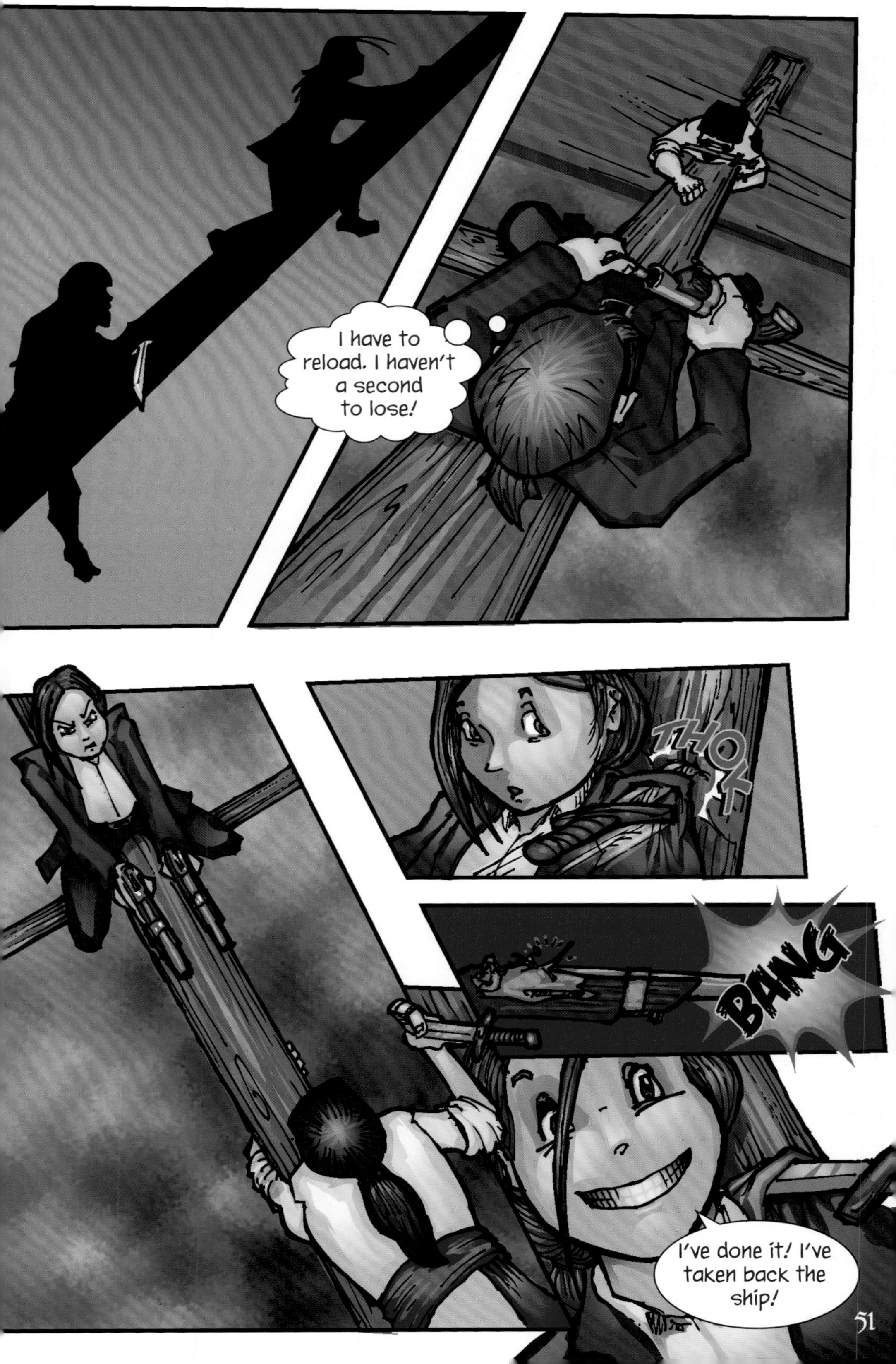
I have to reload. I haven't a second to lose!
THOK
BANG
I've done it! I've taken back the ship!

CHAPTER 5 Captain Silver

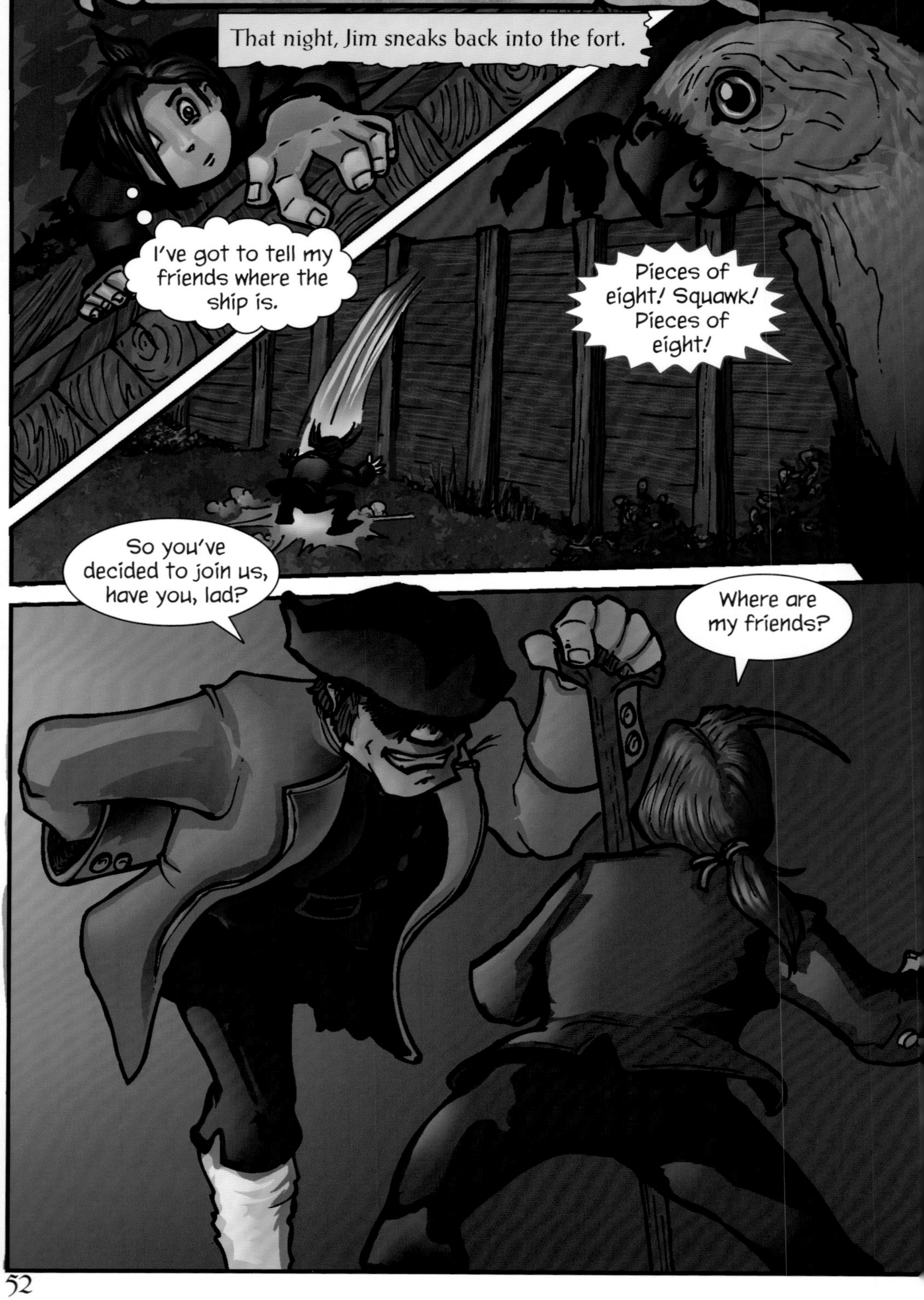
That night, Jim sneaks back into the fort.
I've got to tell my friends where the ship is.
Pieces of eight! Squawk! Pieces of eight!
So you've decided to join us, have you, lad?
Where are my friends?

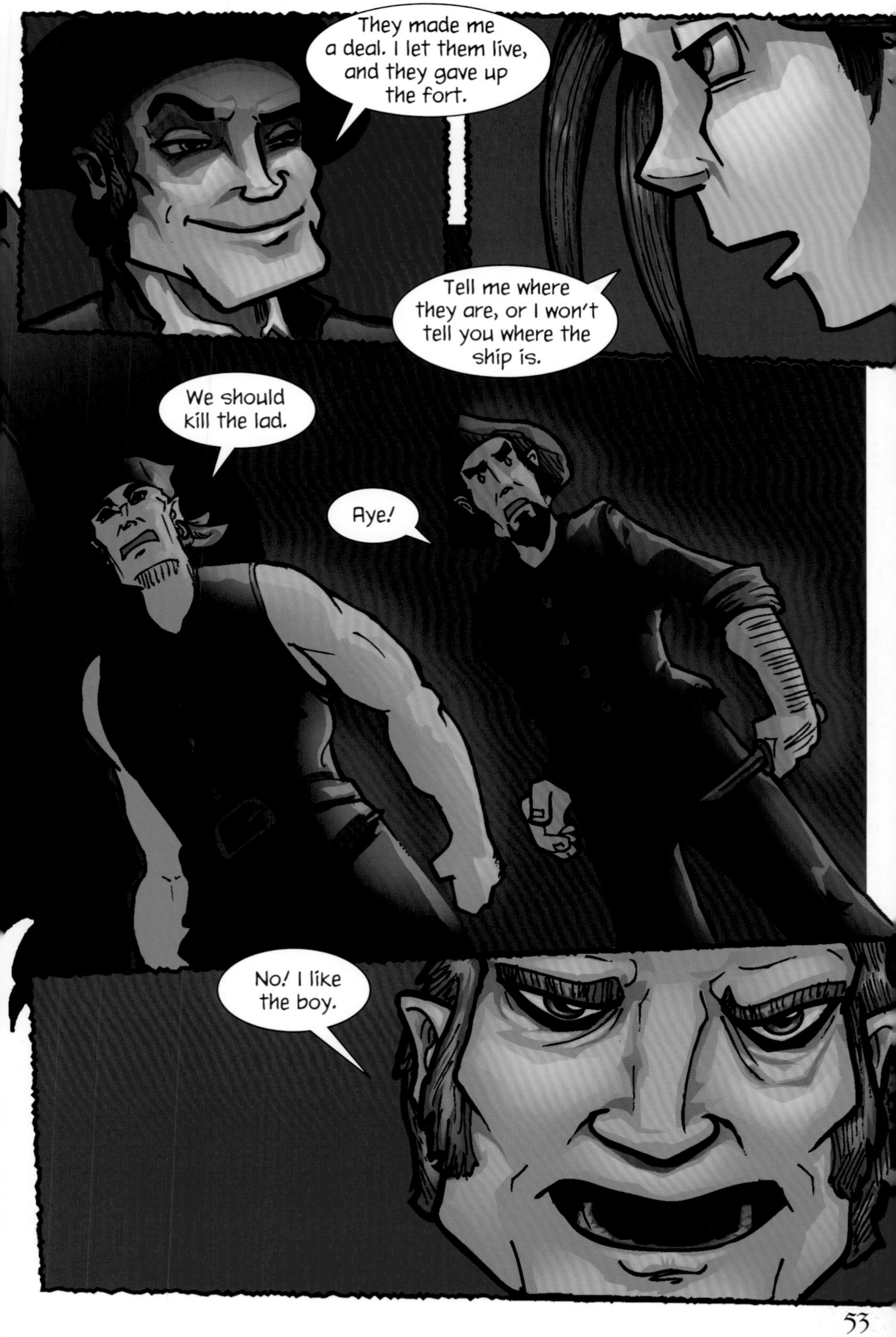
They made me a deal. I let them live, and they gave up the fort.
Tell me where they are, or I won't tell you where the ship is.
We should kill the lad.
Aye!
No! I like the boy.

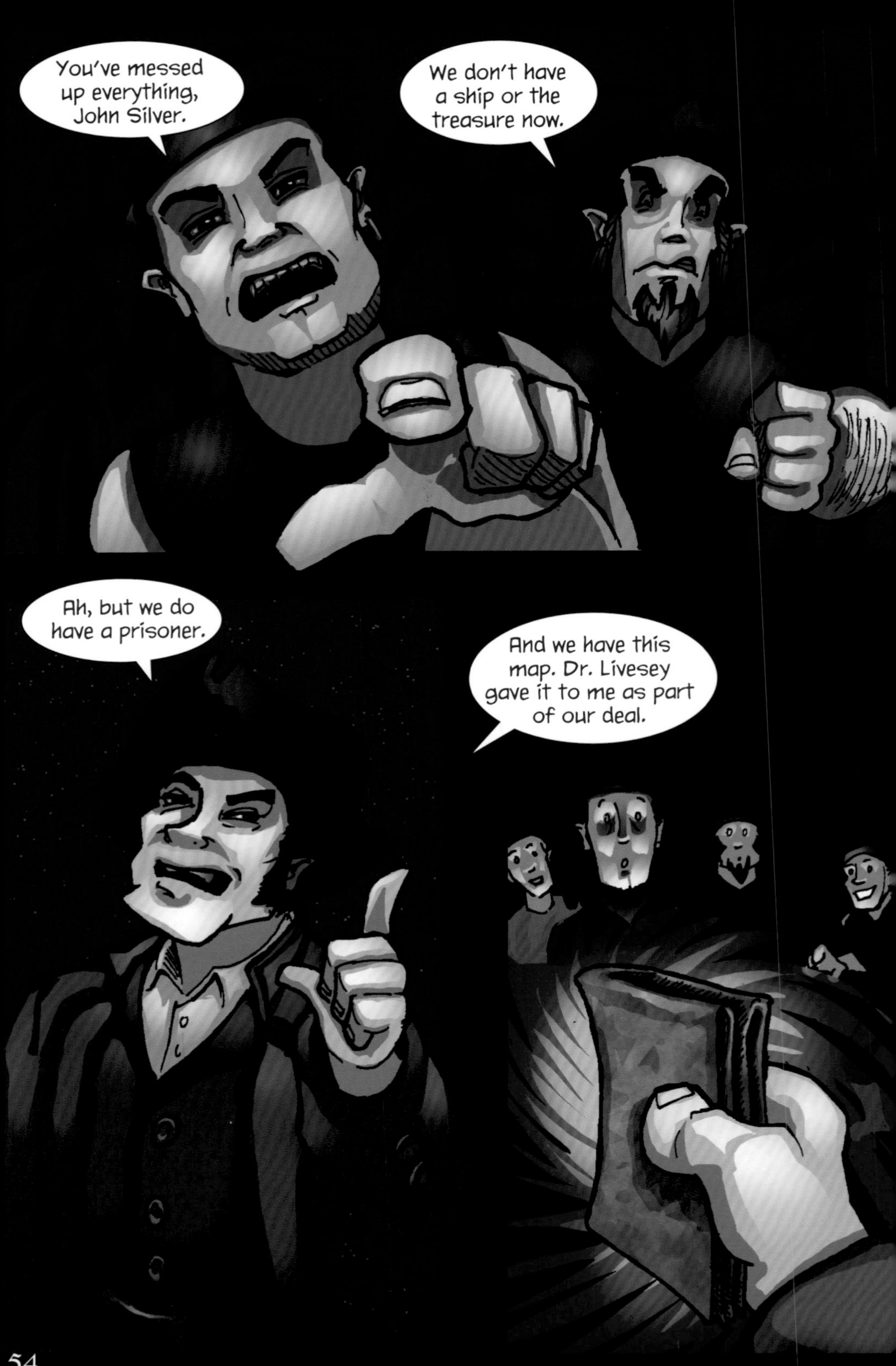
You've messed up everything, John Silver.
We don't have a ship or the treasure now.
Ah, but we do have a prisoner.
And we have this map. Dr. Livesey gave it to me as part of our deal.

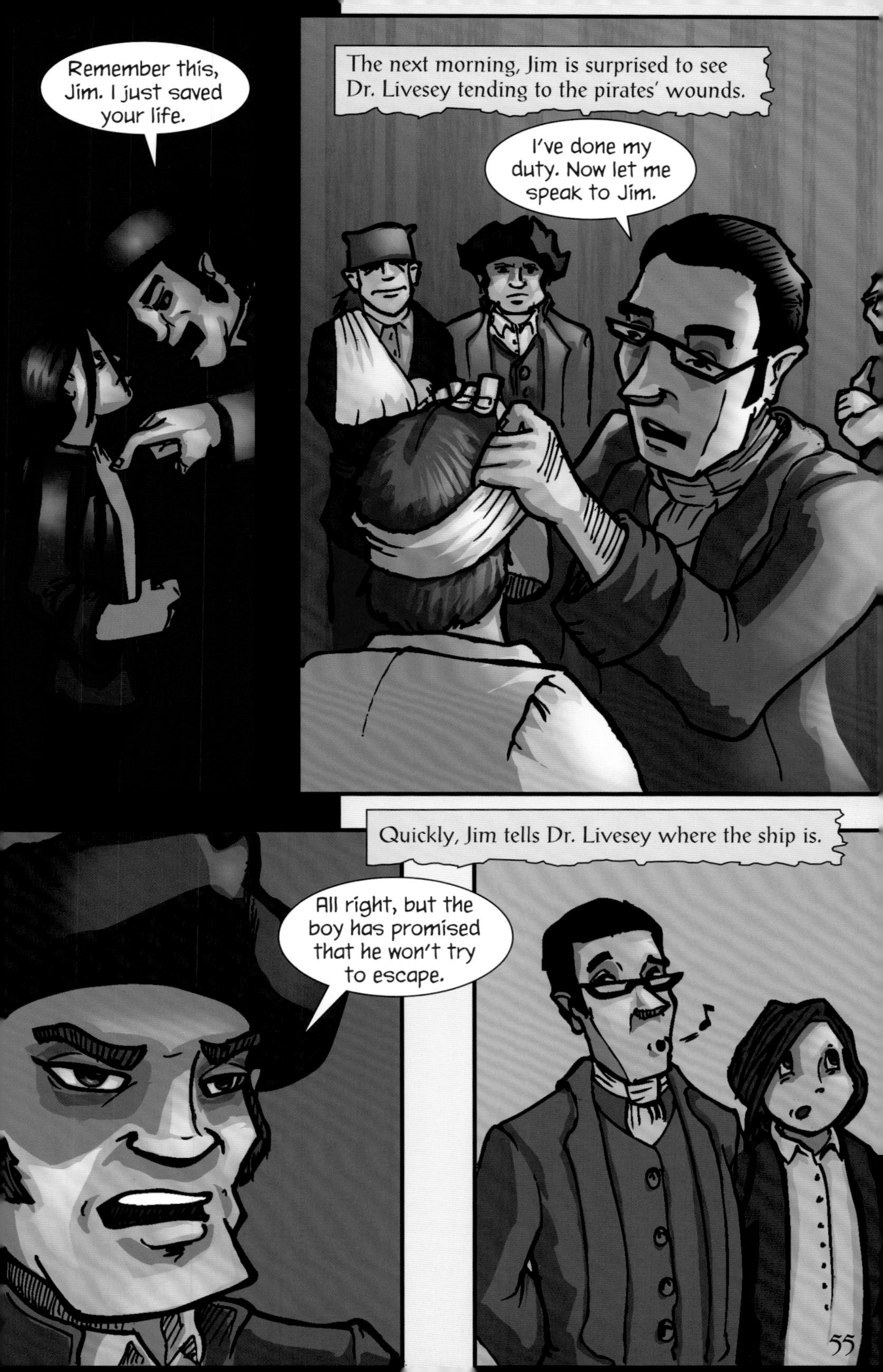

Remember this, Jim. I just saved your life.
The next morning, Jim is surprised to see Dr. Livesey tending to the pirates' wounds.
I've done my duty. Now let me speak to Jim.
Quickly, Jim tells Dr. Livesey where the ship is.
All right, but the boy has promised that he won't try to escape.

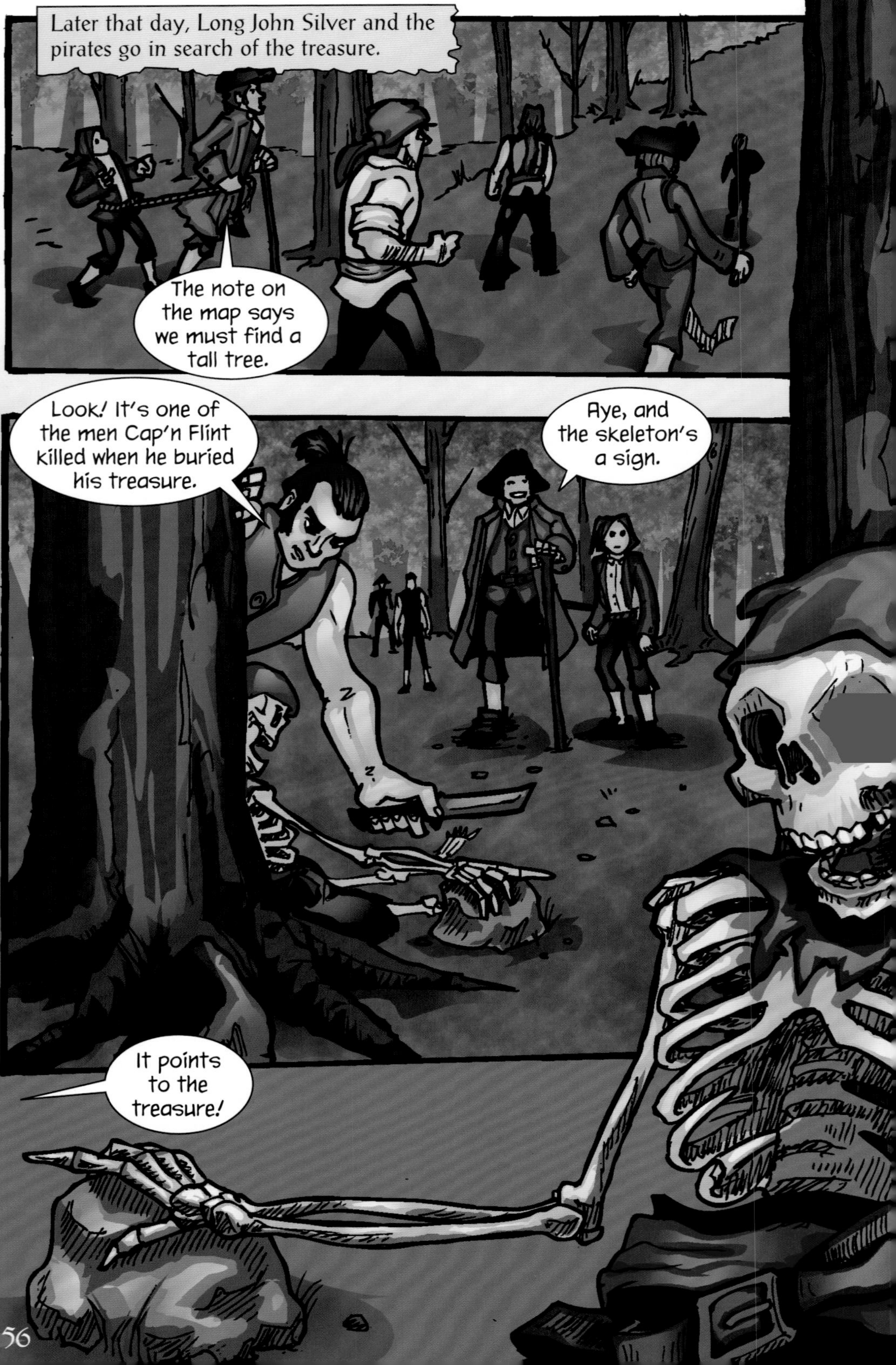
Later that day, Long John Silver and the pirates go in search of the treasure.
The note on the map says we must find a tall tree.
Look! It's one of the men Cap'n Flint killed when he buried his treasure.
Aye, and the skeleton's a sign.
It points to the treasure!

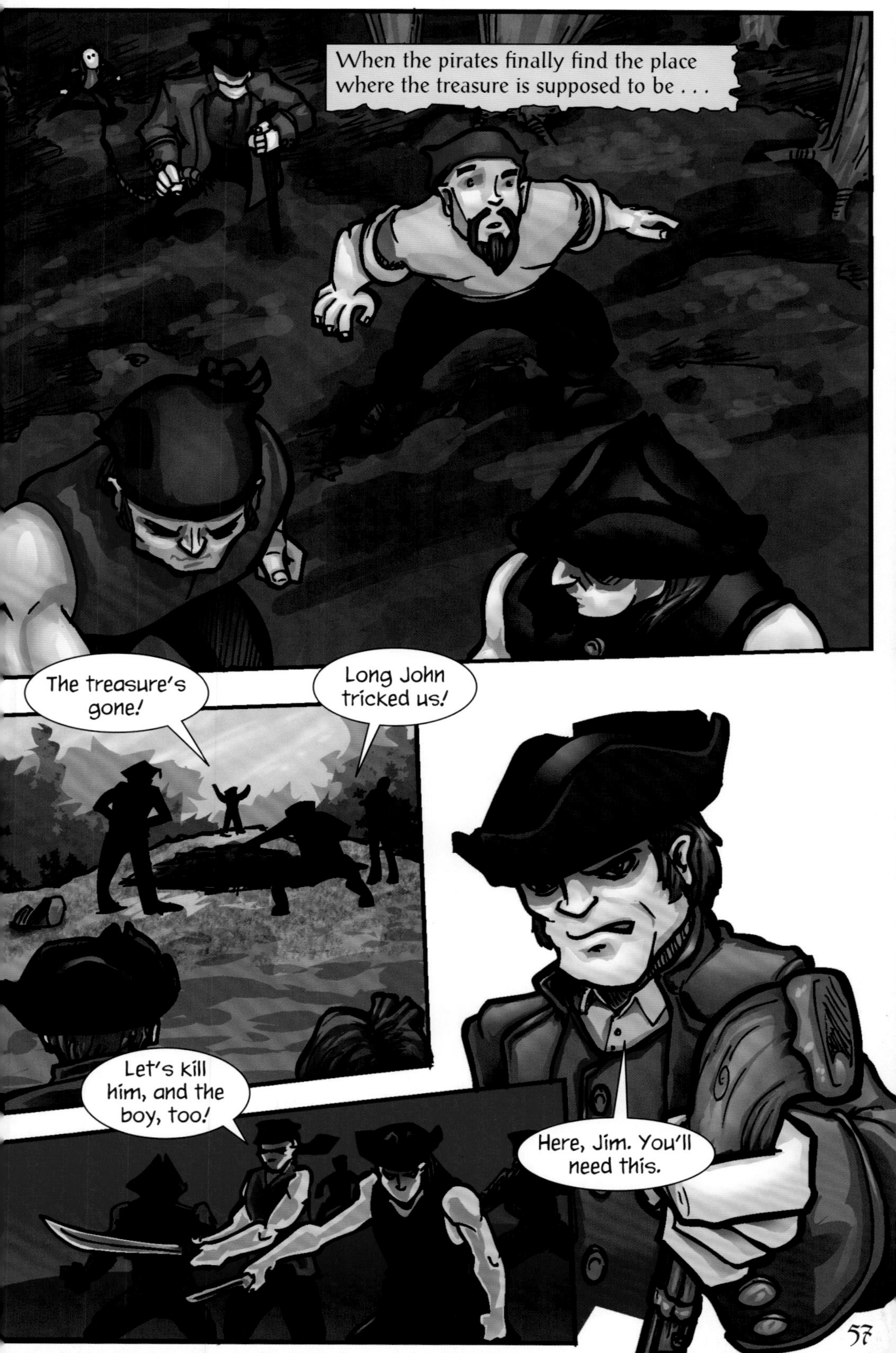
When the pirates finally find the place where the treasure is supposed to be . . .
The treasure's gone!
Long John tricked us!
Let's kill him, and the boy, too!
Here, Jim. You'll need this.

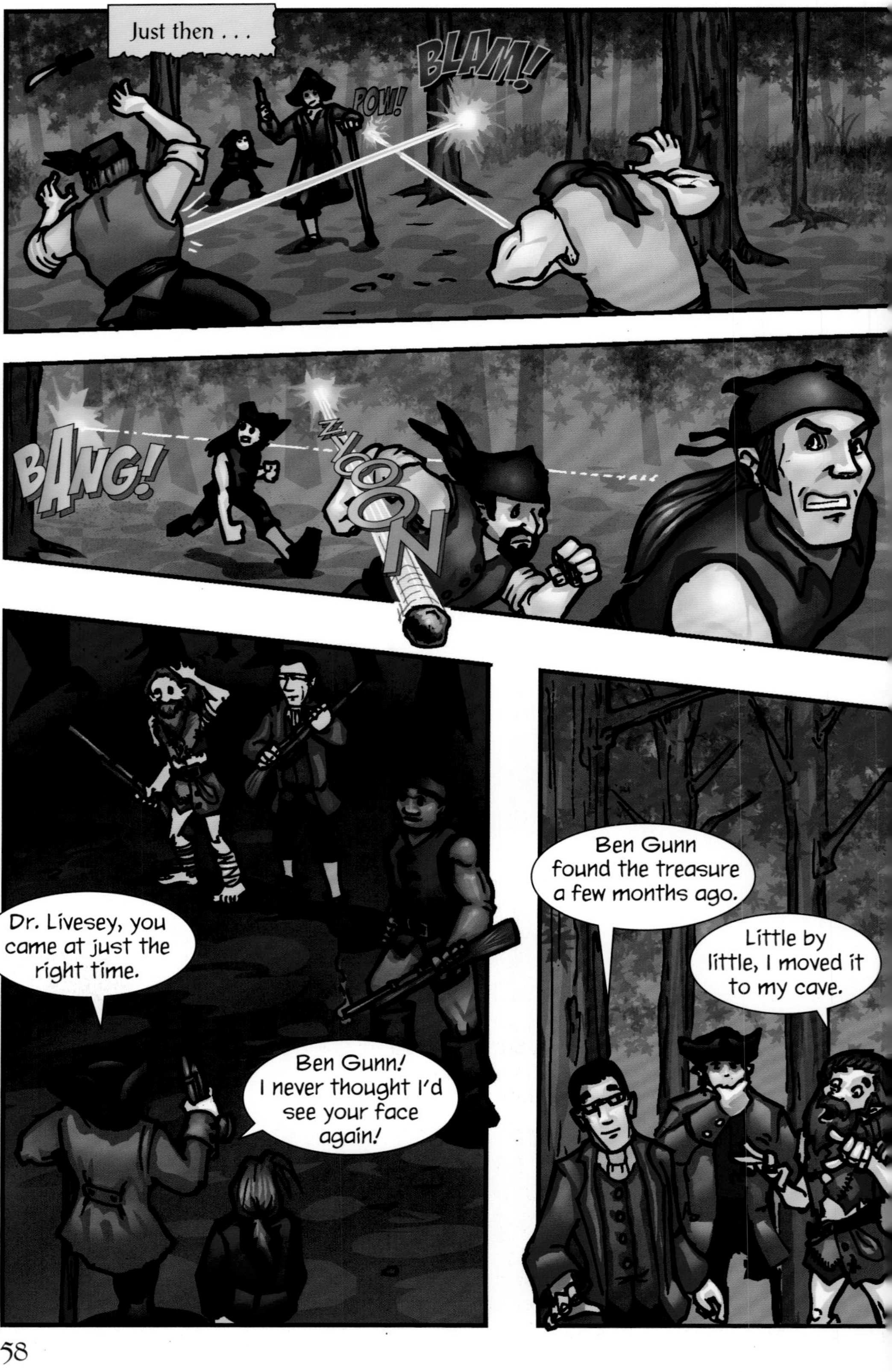
Just then . . .
POW!
BLAM!
BANG!
ZYOOON
Dr. Livesey, you came at just the right time.
Ben Gunn! I never thought I'd see your face again!
Ben Gunn found the treasure a few months ago.
Little by little, I moved it to my cave.

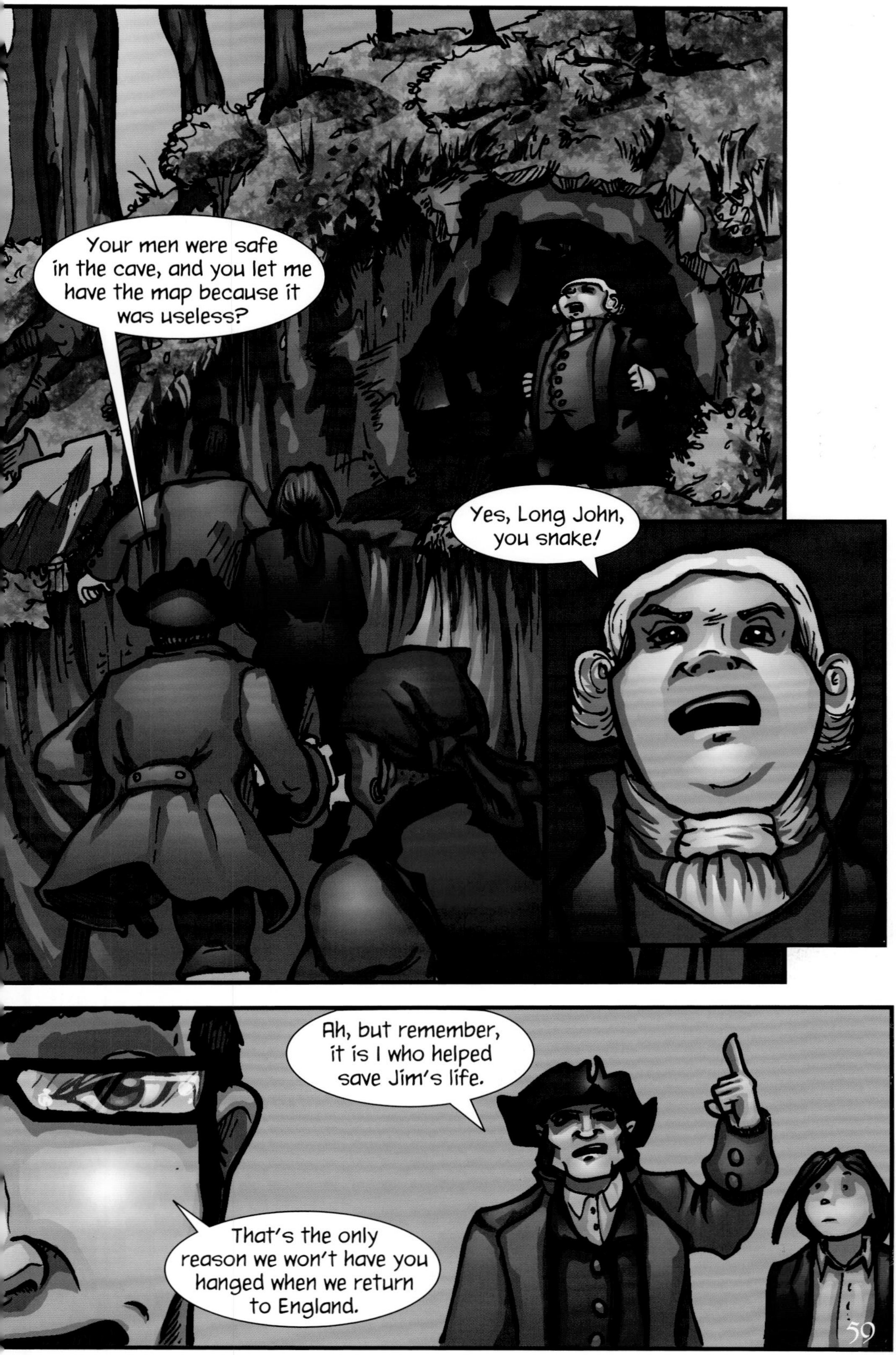
Your men were safe in the cave, and you let me have the map because it was useless?
Yes, Long John, you snake!
Ah, but remember, it is I who helped save Jim's life.
That's the only reason we won't have you hanged when we return to England.

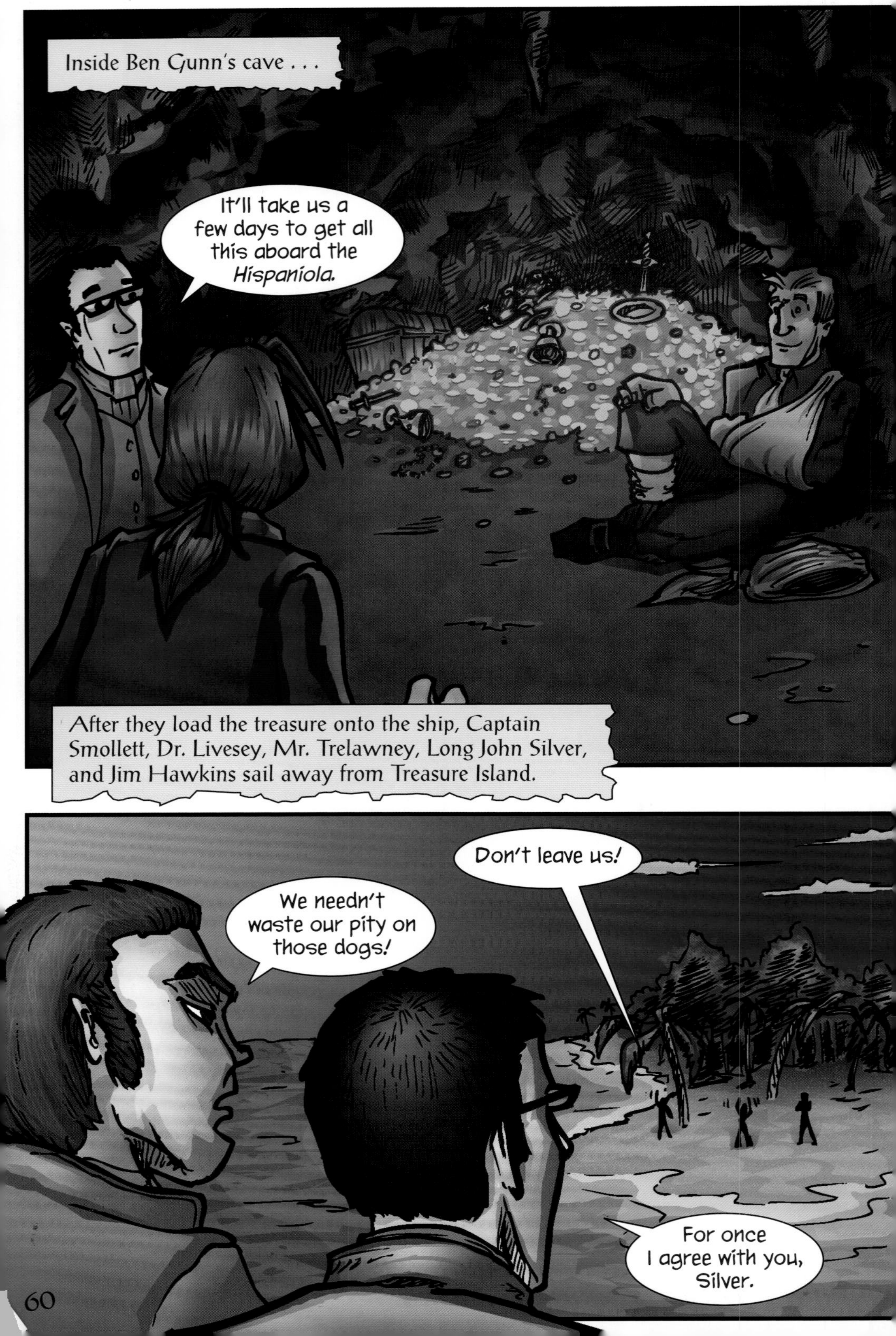
Inside Ben Gunn's cave . . .
It'll take us a few days to get all this aboard the *Hispaniola.*
After they load the treasure onto the ship, Captain Smollett, Dr. Livesey, Mr. Trelawney, Long John Silver, and Jim Hawkins sail away from Treasure Island.
Don't leave us!
We needn't waste our pity on those dogs!
For once I agree with you, Silver.

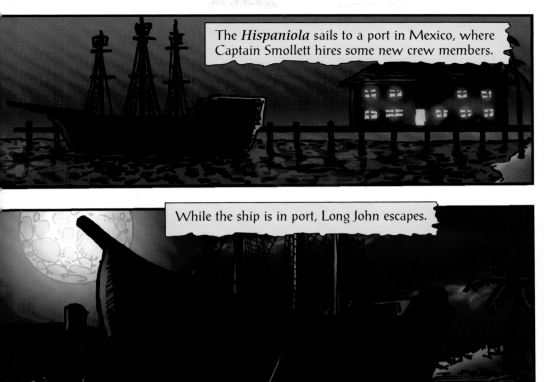

The *Hispaniola* sails to a port in Mexico, where Captain Smollett hires some new crew members.

While the ship is in port, Long John escapes.

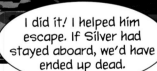

I did it! I helped him escape. If Silver had stayed aboard, we'd have ended up dead.

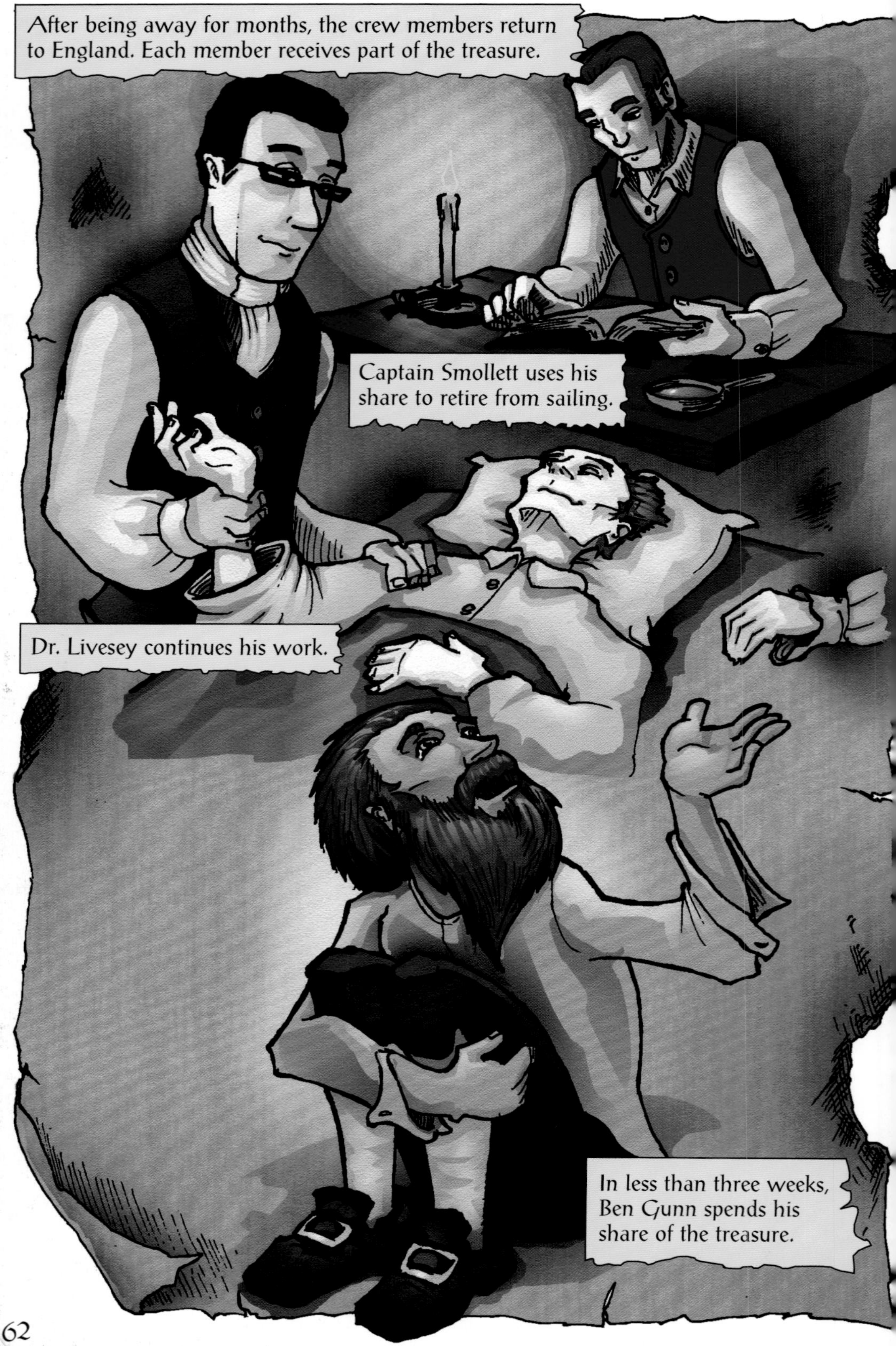
After being away for months, the crew members return to England. Each member receives part of the treasure.
Captain Smollett uses his share to retire from sailing.
Dr. Livesey continues his work.
In less than three weeks, Ben Gunn spends his share of the treasure.

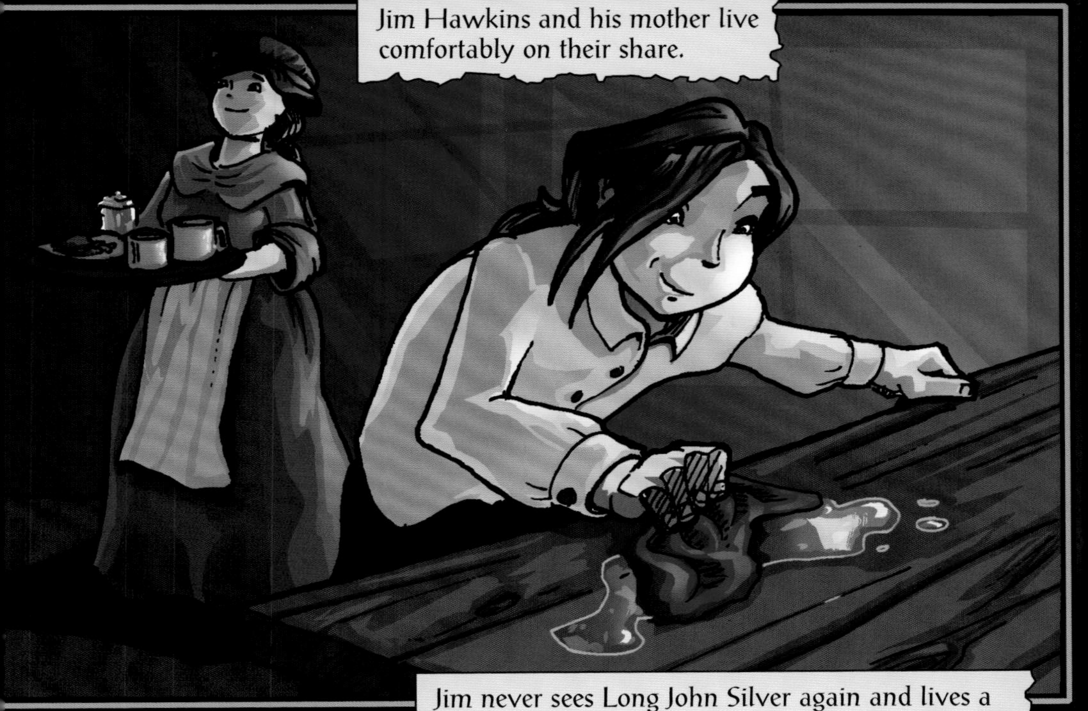
Jim Hawkins and his mother live comfortably on their share.

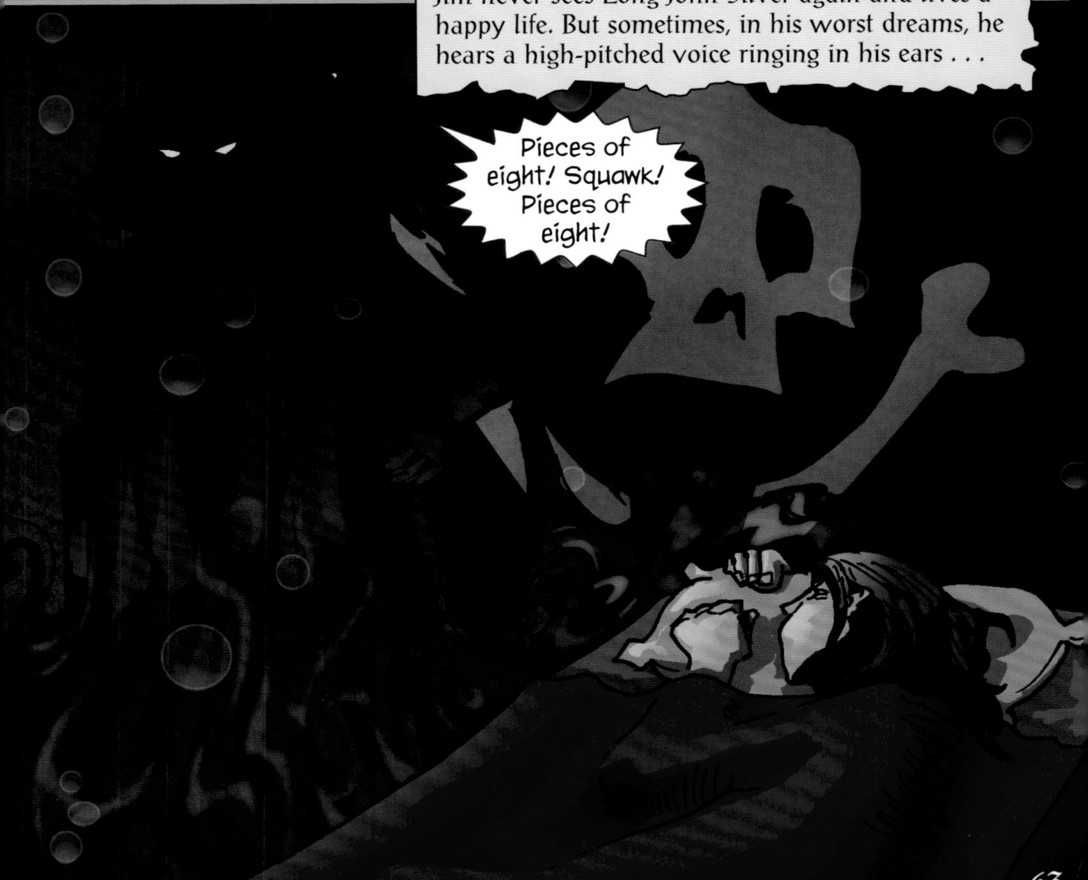
Jim never sees Long John Silver again and lives a happy life. But sometimes, in his worst dreams, he hears a high-pitched voice ringing in his ears . . .
Pieces of eight! Squawk! Pieces of eight!

ABOUT ROBERT LOUIS STEVENSON

Robert Louis Stevenson was born in 1850 in Edinburgh, Scotland. He enjoyed traveling and having adventures. During one family vacation in Scotland, Stevenson and his stepson amused themselves by drawing a treasure map for an imaginary island. The stories he and his stepson told inspired Stevenson to write *Treasure Island.* It was published in 1883. Stevenson's other famous books include *Kidnapped* and *The Strange Case of Dr. Jekyll and Mr. Hyde.* He died in 1894.

ABOUT THE RETELLING AUTHORS

Wim Coleman and Pat Perrin are a married couple who love writing books together. They have written many young adult nonfiction and fiction books, including retellings of classic novels, stories, and myths. They run a scholarship program for Mexican students and live in Guanajuato, Mexico.

ABOUT THE ILLUSTRATOR

Greg Rebis was born in Queens, New York, but grew up mostly in central Florida. After working in civic government, pizza delivery, music retail and proofreading, he eventually landed work in publishing, film and graphics. He currently lives and studies in Rhode Island and still loves art, sci-fi and video games.

GLOSSARY

ashore (uh-SHOR) — on or toward the shore or land

beach (BEECH) — to land a ship on the shore

curiosity (kyur-ee-AHSS-i-tee) — wanting to know more about things

Hispaniola (HISS-span-ee-oh-la) — Captain Smollett's ship

inn (IN) — a small hotel, often with a restaurant

magistrate (MAJ-uh-strate) — a government official or judge who has the power to enforce the law

mate (MAYT) — a friend or person that someone works with

pieces of eight (PEESS-iz uhv ATE) — in pirate times, the Spanish currency was the peso, which was worth eight reales. Sometimes, a pirate would break the peso coin into eight pieces to make change.

request (re-KWEST) — something that is asked for

seaman (SEE-man) — a sailor

shipwrecked (SHIP-rekd) — a ship that has been destroyed at sea

tending to (TEN-ding TOO) — taking care of

truce (TROOS) — an agreement to stop fighting

Background of Treasure Island

In the 1700s, the world of Jim Hawkins was full of sailing ships. People crossed the oceans, transported goods, and explored new lands using wind power and strong ocean currents. In seaside towns, ships were loaded along the wharves, or docks. A captain called his ship "shipshape" or "seaworthy" if it was ready to go to sea. And when the captain yelled "all hands on deck," the crew boarded, ready to work.

Each person on a ship had their own special job to do. Cabin boys, hoping to learn more about sailing, served the captain. The captain steered the ship by turning the ship's tiller. Crew members would lift and lower the heavy sails. To keep the ship in one place, the crew would drop an anchor, or heavy weight. If a ship went adrift, meaning that it floated off course, the crew sometimes stopped it by sailing it onto land, or beaching it. The life of a sailor was hard, and not all crew members made it home alive.

Ships traveled on the "high seas," waters that were not owned by any country. Life at sea was full of danger. A ship could sink in a storm or become shipwrecked. Crews could be stranded on strange islands or coastlines. Pirates could attack. To show they were in command of a ship, pirates would "raise the Jolly Roger," hang a black flag with a skull and crossbones from a high mast.

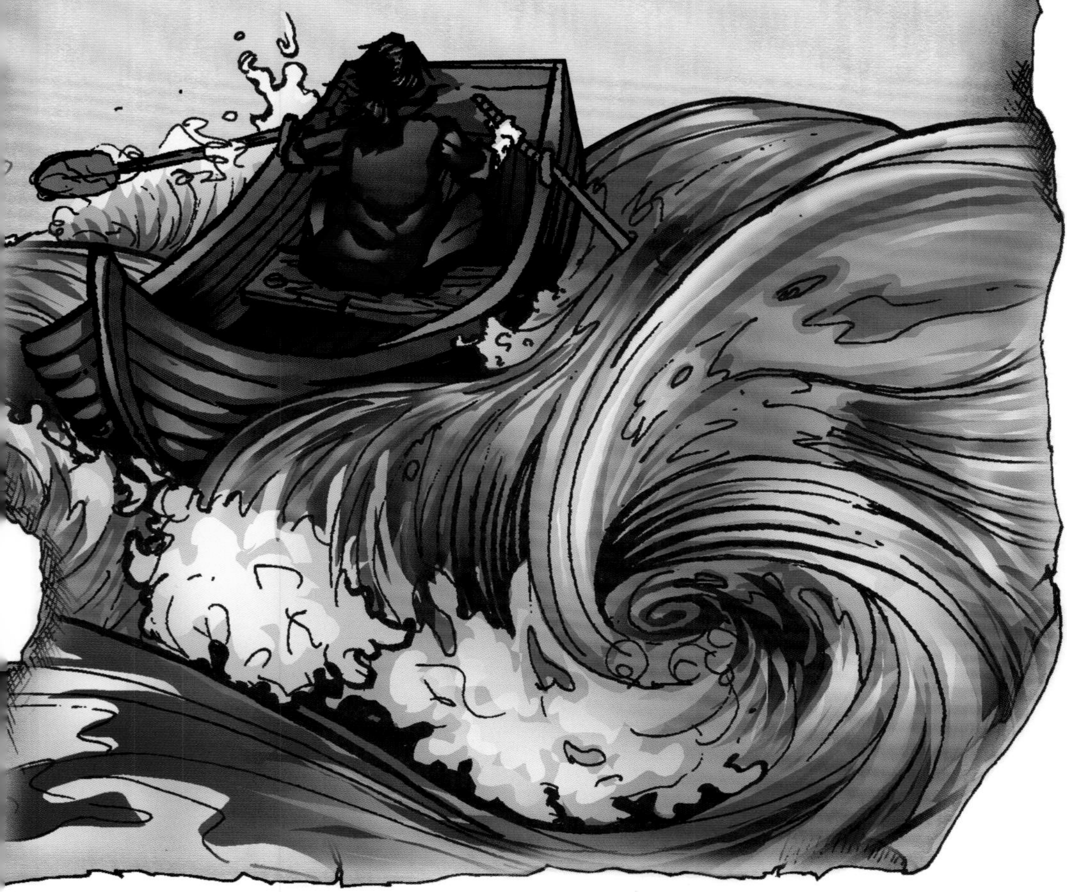

DISCUSSION QUESTIONS

1. Why did Billy Bones die?

2. How did Jim figure out that Long John Silver was the one-legged pirate that Billy Bones told him about?

3. What would you do if you found a buried treasure?

4. Why did Jim sneak onto one of the small boats when the pirates went to look for buried treasure?

WRITING PROMPTS

1. At the end of the story, the pirates flee and the remaining crew members of the *Hispaniola* divide the treasure. How did each person spend the treasure? What does this tell you about each person?

2. Describe your favorite character in *Treasure Island*. Why do you like this character? Would you want to sail on a ship with this person?

3. If you could pick any place in the world to have an adventure, where would you go? Explain how you would get there and what you would discover.

Other Books

ROBIN HOOD
retold by Aaron Shepard and Anne L. Watson
illustrated by Jennifer Tanner
GRAPHIC NOVEL
STONE ARCH

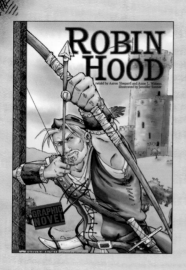

Robin Hood

Robin Hood and his Merrie Men are the heroes of Sherwood Forest. Taking from the rich and giving to the poor, Robin Hood and his loyal followers fight for the downtrodden and oppressed. As they outwit the cruel Sheriff of Nottingham, Robin Hood and his Merrie Men are led on a series of exciting adventures.

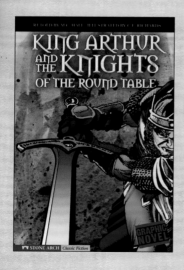

KING ARTHUR AND THE KNIGHTS OF THE ROUND TABLE
GRAPHIC NOVEL
STONE ARCH Classic Fiction

King Arthur and the Knights of the Round Table

In a world of wizards, giants, and dragons, King Arthur and the Knights of the Round Table are the kingdom of Camelot's only defense against the threatening forces of evil. Fighting battles and saving those in need, the Knights of the Round Table can defeat every enemy but one – themselves!

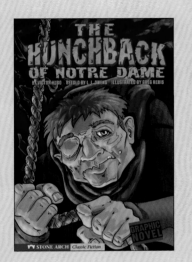

THE HUNCHBACK OF NOTRE DAME
BY VICTOR HUGO RETOLD BY L. L. OWENS ILLUSTRATED BY GREG REBIS
GRAPHIC NOVEL
STONE ARCH Classic Fiction

The Hunchback of Notre Dame

Hidden away in the bell tower of the Cathedral of Notre Dame, Quasimodo is treated like a beast. Although he is gentle and kind, he has the reputation of a frightening monster because of his physical deformities. He develops affection for Esmeralda, a gypsy girl who shows him kindness in return. When the girl is sentenced to an unfair death by hanging, Quasimodo is determined to save her. But those closest to Quasimodo have other plans for the gypsy.

The Adventures of
TOM SAWYER
BY MARK TWAIN RETOLD BY M. C. HALL ILLUSTRATED BY DANIEL STRICKLAND
GRAPHIC NOVEL
STONE ARCH Classic Fiction

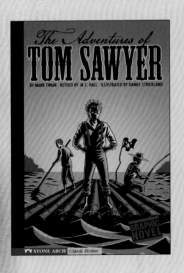

Tom Sawyer

Tom Sawyer is the cleverest of characters, constantly outwitting those around him. Then there is Huckleberry Finn, the envy of the town's schoolchildren because he has the rare gift of complete freedom, never attending school or answering to anyone but himself. After Tom and Huck witness a murder, they find themselves on a series of adventures that leads them to some seriously frightening situations.

Internet Sites

Do you want to know more about subjects related to this book? Or are you interested in learning about other topics? Then check out FactHound, a fun, easy way to find Internet sites.

Our investigative staff has already sniffed out great sites for you!

Here's how to use FactHound:

1. Visit *www.facthound.com*

2. Select your grade level.

3. To learn more about subjects related to this book, type in the book's ISBN number: **1598890506.**

4. Click the **Fetch It** button.

FactHound will fetch the best Internet sites for you!